Thread Twice Cut

A Science Fiction Novel

Bryan Costales

A Fool Church Media Publication

Published by

Fool Church Media
Eugene, Oregon

This novel is a work of fiction. Names, characters, places and incidents either are the product of the author's imagination or are used fictitiously. Other than well known historical people or events, any resemblance to actual persons, living or dead, events or locales is entirely coincidental.

Thread Twice Cut

1st Edition 2017: Fool Church Media
Cover Photograph by Bryan Costales

Softcover ISBN: 978-1-945232-18-3
Epub ISBN: 978-1-945232-19-0
HTML ISBN: 978-1-945232-20-6
Kindle ISBN: 978-1-945232-21-3

Manufactured/Printed in the United States of America

Table Of Contents

Table Of Contents (cont.)

Dedication

Terry Costales

Acknowledgments

Special thanks must go to my wife Terry Costales who read through the many drafts of this book without complaint, and who provided inspiring insightful feedback. Thanks to George Jansen whose own writing has inspired me so much over the years. Final thanks to Allison Wright who provided a professional edit within my budget via fiverr.

Cowards die many times
before their deaths;
The valiant never taste of
death but once.
Of all the wonders that I yet
have heard,
It seems to me most strange
that men should fear;
Seeing that death, a necessary
end,
Will come when it will come.

William Shakespeare
"Julius Caesar", Act 2 scene 2

Prologue: Origin Of Angels

145 Days Since the Invasion

Wind whistled in my ears with the sound of a waterfall, yet not a drop of water was in sight. Just dry, cracked and crevassed dirt —the result of another oven heated day. Sand skittered and rattled metal hard against an ancient, dry, faded-red, gas pump, the price still a cheap $159.99 per gallon; a hand written sign still held with yellow tape to its face. The old station had collapsed into red, white and dirt, abstract metal wreckage. Bullet holes, signs of rust and that blackened charred smell of bygone fire. The highway beyond the station was still paved, but with thin brown weeds growing tall through almost mathematically parallel cracks.

My feet ached from too much walking in worn shoes, step after step, trudging too far for too long, alone.

Sure, I feel sorry for myself, but —well, there had been Nancy in Needles, ten years older than me and sick with the Cough, soft and warm she was, and good to make love to until she passed. Now me, suffering from an infection in my finger because of a damned cut I got when I pounded her cross into hard dirt using a two-by-four with rusty nails. I couldn't think of a thing to say over her grave there at the edge of town among so many other nameless graves; among the anonymous dead, among the no longer remembered, among those who should probably have never been born. Her grave was embarrassingly shallow, dug in desert dirt too hard to dig. It must have been over 115 degrees that day, so hot even soaking in the muddy Colorado River brought no relief whatsoever. I used my dirty hand to wipe sticky sweat from my forehead and pulled my straw hat back down to protect my head. The sun behind me cast a long shadow.

My eyes were sharply peeled for rattlesnakes, the nasty green ones. I noticed something in the distance moving toward me. It looked like a robot. It was walking, no make that trudging, east in the earliest of amber morning light. The robot walked on eight legs like a spider. Silver and shiny in places, but mostly rusted overall with faded lines of blue and mustard safety yellow. Two arms, one raised in greeting. Botched, I thought, when I saw pieces missing as it drew near. "What are you?" I asked. I was ready to run. The spider was the size of a car.

"Traffic control unit 23," it stopped walking and said, once again in English, then once in Spanish, once in Chinese, once in guttural Russian.

"Just speak in English," I said.

I heard something tick inside it, or maybe that was just the sound of metal changing shape in the morning heat.

"Okay, English," it said, and with a whir it settled to the ground. "I run low on power."

Eight equally spaced legs folded. Each foot had once been padded, but the padding had worn off leaving a patch of shiny metal between two thin patches of rubber. Its body was cobbled together from parts of computers and metal salvaged from assorted machines. I noticed an old iPhone inside a tangle of wires. A huge phone so much larger than the iRing I got for my 45th birthday, the day before all those airliners crashed, the day before all those people were shot on the streets of DC, the day after that alien ship landed. Before everything fell apart. Before the Cough.

"There's no power where I came from," I said, uncertain if I should speak to the eyes or not, because the robot had no obvious ears.

"Are you a threat to me?" the robot asked.

"No," I said. "I'm just glad for any conversation at all. I will help you find power if I can."

The robot whirred again and rose on its legs. "The man that built me warned me to say I was a traffic control robot and to say I was running out of power to avoid threats from bad humans. But I have seen zero humans at all for two weeks. You are the first one I have found alive."

I walked around it to see what else I might find. Old coffee tins, headlights off cars, dials from an airplane cockpit, and parts from a precision machine shop. Here and there I smelled something like spices or weeds. "You mean you were playing possum?"

"What's a possum?" it asked. Its voice seemed to always come from the side closest to me. Its voice was high-pitched and crackly as if from small speakers.

147 Days

I awoke to a whistle, a continuous, high-pitched bubbly sound. Confused, I rolled over off my pad onto hard, rocky ground and pushed myself up. My arm, the one with the bad finger, hurt all the way up to my elbow. The robot had steam rising off its platform, white steam against a cloudless blue sky.

The robot pivoted its eyes to look at me. "I boiled water," it said.

"For coffee?"

"I have no coffee. Look in the green box. There may be tea in it."

I pulled on my boots, wishing I had clean socks without holes, and walked over to the robot. On the side nearest me was a thin hot plate with a teapot on top, the two held together with a large C-clamp. The whistling stopped, but the sight of steam still drifting cloud-like from the nozzle thrilled me. I looked around the surface of the robot and found the green antique tin box with the words, "Smiths Oil" on it. Inside the box was a single, restaurant-style ceramic cup and a tin of tea bags all padded with shredded paper. Black tea, mint tea, and Chinese tea —I actually had to choose. I remembered the Raman noodles in my backpack and smiled.

That was the best breakfast I had eaten in over a month. As I ate, the robot introduced itself.

"The man called me Ralph," the robot told me.

"Hi, Ralph," I said, just like I used to back in AA. I smacked my lips. I could use a stiff drink right now. But I wasted my last bottle of vodka trying to disinfect my finger as I walked uphill and out of Needles. Lots of damn good that did. I made a fist and my finger screamed back at me.

"But Ralph isn't my real name," the robot spider said. "It was a name made up by the man who rebuilt me. I was originally a flying machine sent here to fix people."

The robot showed me a map projected in the air just the way my ring used to. The map showed black dots scattered all over the place.

"I'm from another planet. The people who built me sent a diplomatic party to your planet and inadvertently caused the pandemic that is killing everyone. Once the people from my planet discovered what they had done, they sent machines like me here to cure everyone. But your people thought we were an invasion and shot us all down."

I laughed. I couldn't help it. Of all the fucked-up stupid things for me to stumble across, the worst was a robot with delusions. "Prove it," I said.

"Look at the map," it said and made the map larger as if that might make it more true. "We are the yellow dot. That black dot to your left is a shot-down ship. I have already found four shot-down ships. When one of our power sources is damaged it explodes into a huge ball of heated energy that burns its way down, thousands of meters into the dirt. The first two dots had no ship, just large lakes, each bigger than a town, now filled with steaming water. The last two were just huge bottomless pits, scorched black on the inside with broken ends of pipes spilling water that turned to steam."

"There's another dot near here," I said, and pointed at a dot. "Just a little way south."

"It is possible there will be an intact ship there. But I have little hope."

I stepped back and crossed my arms. I winced and then uncrossed them. "So what happened to your ship?"

Ralph turned off the map. "I was shot down, but my core was not destroyed. It was ejected for safety. A young boy found my core and carried it to the man. The boy told me the man was the smartest man he had ever met. The man rebuilt me into what you see. And then, soldiers came and blew up my ship."

The robot Ralph actually sounded sad.

"That man," Ralph continued, "installed me into this robot. Soon after that he died of the Cough. I didn't have my ship so I could not save him. Before he died, he told me the boy had also died of the Cough."

"Sorry," I said and put my hand on Ralph, but it felt like putting my hand on the hood of a car. A used car with cracked paint. Like that old clunker, my first car, a used blue Zeus with its terrible batteries that caused it to suck gas, but it had really comfortable seats. The back seat of that car was where I first made love to my wife before she was my wife. Sure Ralph felt like a car, but I was glad that feeling of warm metal could bring back memories of better times. What the hell, I decided I might as well stick with him, for a while anyway.

Later that morning we walked together south. I walked next to Ralph as if he was a friend, but he wasn't a friend, was he? He was just a machine.

We walked until sunset, then I dined on hot Raman noodles for dinner and finally ate both the Ho Hos and found them sweeter than I expected, almost too sweet. I finally slept, while Ralph kept watch. I don't think I dreamed.

148 Days

Dawn and tea and Raman noodles and no hope for a sweet dessert ever again. I walked with Ralph toward a black dot on a map, a small spot of black floating in the air over a moving metal spider. It was certainly not something real. Still, one nice thing about a heavy walking machine was that there was no sign of the green rattlesnakes. They must have all fled from the squeaking metal feet.

"What's your real name?" I asked him. "I mean if the man named you Ralph, you must have a name of your own."

"Angel," he said, "or that's the nearest meaning I can find to my name in the languages of your planet. And that is just a close match. Nothing else is closer."

"How does your name sound in your own language?"

Ralph made a sound that was a cross between a gargle and a yodel with a buzz and pop mixed in, but vaguely musical with its own internal rhythm.

"I can't say that," I said.

We walked silently for a while because my whole arm was now aching from my infected finger. I tried to hang it down my side, but it hurt that way, so I put my hand in my pocket and that hurt worse. I found that by resting it on Ralph while we walked, it hurt less. When I had the chance, I rolled up my sleeve to look at what hurt and saw the black lines of blood poisoning. I tapped on the black veins thinking they would be numb, but instead they hurt like hell. I had to bite my lip to keep myself from shouting. Ralph didn't appear to notice my pain.

We walked along that narrow dirt road until we reached and passed two skeletons in a ditch wearing tattered army uniforms, rifles still clutched in their skeletal hands. "I wonder what they were guarding," I said. But the robot had already moved ahead of me.

It surprised me how real the skeletons looked, not like Halloween skeletons, but real bone with bits of dried flesh still stuck in places. I shook both canteens, but they were both empty.

Next we passed a large military truck on its side and rusting, its fabric top torn into soiled ribbons. To the east, black vultures circled in the sky, high and slow, almost majestically. To the west I heard coyotes yip just beyond sight somewhere over the next bare rise. Grey clouds had moved in so the sun wasn't so overwhelmingly fucking hot. No water in the truck either. I kept walking through midday.

We crested a low hill and in a clearing on the other side was an odd-looking black rectangle that appeared to be about the size of a shipping container. I stopped and shaded my eyes with my good hand to study it. "Is that one of your ships?" I asked.

"No," Ralph said. "Perhaps a ship is inside."

As we descended, the shipping container grew larger. It became a much larger building than I had first thought. It grew more impressive as we approached it. At least two dozen graves with dead soldier helmets hung on crosses filled an area next to it. Only one cross had a name, a woman named, Ellen Samson, but none of the other crosses had names. I tried to imagine why that might be but came up empty. Then I remembered Needles and whispered, "Ah."

Parked near the container was a water truck. I turned the nozzle and water rushed out. Very hot and grey but I drank it anyway. It tasted stale but I didn't care. I rubbed water into my hair and tried to soak my clothes to cool me off. But the heat of the water prevented any cooling effect. Briefly refreshed, I hurried to catch up with Ralph.

Now that we were close, that container looked human-made. Like a big hangar for airplanes, it towered over me. Maybe it was a secret place for experiments. Maybe this was the rumored Area 51, but no, that was in Nevada. The valley was dead quiet except for the metal spider clanking beside me. The air smelled like dirt. The graves looked sad.

At the far end of the huge hangar we rounded the corner and found a tall roll-up door that was rolled down. At least this side of the building was in shade and the temperature was a hair cooler. I shoved my hat up to help cool my forehead, but that made little difference —I was still too hot. The air itself was too hot. I pushed the "up" button with my good hand and felt it click, but nothing happened. So I looked for a manual override and found a hand crank handle in a glass case with the words, "In emergency, break glass," on it.

It took a long time to hand crank the door up, so long that I had to rest there in the baking shade before finishing. I couldn't remember ever tiring that fast before.

Inside the hangar, just a dozen feet in was a black box much smaller than the hangar, about two dozen feet long, maybe twelve feet tall, and a bit less wide. It was in the shape of a black toaster with rounded corners on top. Its color was flat black, so dark that it seemed to almost absorb light.

"An intact ship," Ralph said matter-of-factly. "I will need your help now."

But I felt sick to my stomach and my arm felt like hell. "I think I need to lie down for a while first," I said and collapsed hard onto building's floor. I tried to barf, but I was too dry so I just gagged briefly. I felt like I was running a fever. I shivered and couldn't stop myself. Despite the heat I now felt cold. "I hope this isn't the Cough," I said, and curled up into a ball.

"You're not coughing," Ralph said.

I laid my head down on that dirty concrete floor. I dreamed hard and in unbelievably vivid colors. My dog Yukon, a female German shepherd, ran through a gentle blue surf chasing a glowing, fire red Frisbee, her tags tinkling clearly even from that distance. Every girlfriend I ever had was lined up on bleachers facing the surf and cheering my wife on as she swam in an effort to beat the dog to that floating red frisbee. My children hovered over me like butterflies, tiny wings beating the air fast like hummingbirds, my son bright blue, my daughter pale yellow. The sweetest aroma caused me to look in the kitchen. It was empty, deserted, quiet but for the whispering of a refrigerator. I opened the refrigerator door and found it filled with stacks and stacks of identical yogurt cartons. Every one of them vanilla.

149 Days

Ralph nudged me with one metal foot to wake me up. I saw it was daylight out again. I sat up and wasn't as dizzy as I had been the night before, but continued shivering despite the warmth. "I think I still have a bad fever," I said.

"If you help me, I can cure you," Ralph said.

"Okay," I said, and used his metal body to pull myself up. I noticed my legs wobbled of their own accord. My old man legs, I thought, how old was I anyway? Forty, forty-two? More like forty-seven! Jesus, my birthday had passed without notice.

"I opened the port on my ship," Ralph said, "but I cannot reach my core because it is hidden underneath me."

An opening appeared in the side of the giant toaster. Inside the opening a pale pink light illuminated an internal white shelf. The shelf's shape reminded me of an old-time milk shake machine from when I was a kid. My mom used to mix up healthy milk shakes using fresh fruit for flavoring. My wife only ever made smoothies in a blender using frozen fruit.

Ralph tapped the edge of itself with a camera eye a quarter turn away from me. "Just under here," he said.

I squatted and crawled underneath. I felt too fucking good there on my back. I eased my head down on the cool concrete and sighed.

His underpart was stained and splattered with mud and oil and something with fur that smelled dead. I found a small metal plate with a wing bolt holding it closed. My chest hurt worse and a throbbing ache ran down my left leg. I could only work the wing bolt loose with my good hand. The wing bolt felt like it was covered in sticky honey, but that was probably only melted paint or plastic. For some reason, that simple task wore me out. I laid my head back down and rested. When I woke up again, the light outside was the bright of midday. I laid on my back under the wing bolt hole. I felt the wing bolt resting on my chest. I reached up with my good hand and rotated a round piece of metal to one side. The metal piece was stiff, but I managed to swing it just enough out of the way.

Everything had a fuzzy cast to it. I blinked my eyes, but that didn't help. A beautifully complex small cylinder about the size of a tall soup can lowered out of the hole. It glowed with a soft white internal light and felt comfortably warm to my hand. It was so internally complex it was hard to look at, despite being fuzzy. "I got it," I said, but Ralph didn't answer. I realized I must have removed his power, or maybe his brain, and now held it in my hand. It was much heavier than I expected, and it smelled like, of all things, a barbecue sauce.

I crawled out from under the robot and used one of its legs to pull myself back up to standing. The hole in the toaster was right there, inches from my face. I slid the soup can into the hole and it vanished, quickly sucked down. The inner black door whooshed closed. Then the outer door snapped silently shut.

I felt a red hot pain in my chest and arms. I couldn't breathe. My mouth felt shrunken down into a straw-sized hole. I fell over backward, and wheezed as my head hit the concrete. The world moved in agonizing slow motion, but I couldn't move, not a muscle. My heart, I thought. "Help," I said, but my mouth only whistled. I knew in that moment I was dying. Fuck it, I thought. But really, no regrets, none. Well maybe just one.

Goodbye my dear, sweet wife. Goodbye, my darling children. Goodbye, Ralph the tin man.

Fire in my chest and arms. Suffocation. Darkness.

Day 1

Darkness but a voice spoke. "I have repaired you." The voice was deep and full, almost as if God himself had spoken. A kind voice, a caring voice, an understanding voice. "I have inserted a small memory device in your brain. This was done so that when you next die, I can bring you back with your memories intact. No matter what, from now on I will always be able to bring you back to life."

I couldn't think of anything to say. I had no idea who I was or where I was. I knew I must be dreaming, but it didn't feel like a dream. Then something black lifted up and off of me and it floated away a short distance. It floated there, stock still, looking like a floating black toaster —whatever a toaster was.

The black thing spoke again, "You lacked a memory device in your brain when you died so I could not restore most of your higher memories. I am sorry."

"Who am I?"

The black thing settled silently back down to the dirt a dozen paces distant. "You never told me your name so I cannot tell it back to you. But you did tell me that you were married and that your wife and two children died."

I tried to remember being married but couldn't. "It's all gone," I said. I felt sad but couldn't understand why.

"You called me Ralph before you died, but my real name translated into your language is Angel."

"You don't look like an angel." I tried to picture an angel in my mind, but I came up empty.

"The device I placed in your brain is not just memory, it is an artificial life capable of recording all your senses too. Your every experience stored in absolute detail, even better than you can remember them yourself."

"Does it have a name too?"

"In your language it could be called Soul."

I rubbed my chin and noticed my hand. It was a young man's hand. I gazed at it and wondered how that could be. I looked at the Angel Ralph and said, "I'm the only one here without a name."

The Angel lifted again. I noticed high in the sky beyond it, hundreds, no, thousands of meteors burning down through the sky. All of them at different angles and in many different directions. "What are those?" I asked with a glance at the Angel. "It looks like a movie version of an alien invasion." But then I realized I had no idea what a movie was.

"I told my planet how three humans here saved me, and how all three gave their lives to restore me. My planet refused to send any more help because of the way we were shot down. But now they have sent more Angels. Smaller ones, but they are just as capable as I am. We will find and heal as many of you humans as we can. We cannot let this civilization die."

"You said I'll never die."

The Angel rose up again. It paused there, far above my head, and said, "Never permanently. We cannot allow it. No human will ever be allowed to die again."

I watched it fly up and away. I watched it fly until it was just a dot among thousands of black dots peppering the sky. "Bye, Ralph," I said. "I mean Angel."

"Thank you," the words spoke in my mind. It was like telepathy, but I knew it was the memory, the Soul, that Angel had put into my brain.

"You are the only human on Earth that can call me Ralph."

"Oh," I said. "But now you're called Angel." But this time there was no answer.

I had a long way to walk, I knew. I now felt healthy and young enough to walk all the way west.

And if no one was alive there then up north and even up to where it snowed if that became necessary. "How about that," I said and smiled. Then, oddly, I missed the wife I couldn't remember and the kids I never knew. It was like remembering and being sad about shadows. Imagine that, me getting to live forever and them dead. Whoever they were.

I ran to the top of the hill, and it felt good to run. I wasn't breathing hard at all. In the distance I could see a road, wavering water-like in the heat. How could I know that was a road? I felt as if I could run all the way down to it.

Off to my left a rattlesnake rattled harshly on a distant flattened boulder. I watched it rattle its alarm for me to come no closer and realized that the snake and I shared something. Neither of us had a name.

"Unless," I said to the snake, "I call myself Rattle. Then we will both share a name."

The snake stopped rattling and curled on the warm rock. It scales glistened beige-green.

I started down the hill and onward toward the road. "Rattle," I said as I walked. "A good name."

The air was hot and dry, no wind, not a speck, not a cloud in the Angel-dotted sky. Silent, not even the distant yapping of coyotes. Silent except for the crunching of my steps, one after the other —forever.

Puppet: 300 Years Later

My butt rested on a soft bench that moved slightly side-to-side under me, not so much swaying as both bouncing and swaying, as if I was on a kid's carnival ride. A chilled breeze made me shiver. I tried to open my eyes but they were struck shut. My nose was partly plugged, so I sniffed in hard, and then out harder. Once my nose was clear the stink surprised me. No, not a bad smell, but more a mixture of odors I couldn't pin down, cheese maybe, or sweat, or flowers. And all around was the buzzing of conversations and distant music, none of which I could recognize or understand.

For a moment I thought I had passed out at the circus. But then I remembered that poor lion and the airliner crashing into me. Had my death been a drug induced illusion? And if so, where was I? The last thing I remembered was the smell of greasepaint, a mirror with a picture of me as a kid tucked into the frame, and that lion shivering in its cage.

A cold nose and wet tongue of a dog sniffed my ear, and then licked it.

I used my hands to force my eyes open. An amazingly beautiful woman turned away as if to walk off. I got a glimpse of her red hair and skintight dress, and her smooth backside and long legs. I blinked to clear my vision.

Was I still stoned? How strong had that weed been? Was I still wearing a clown nose? No I had taken that off.

I was seated on a bench, of some sort, parallel to a pure white roadway filled to overflowing with costumed people. I felt the dog sniff me again. "Stop sniffing me," I said.

The dog pulled its head back. A large dog, its head level with mine.

Two tall women stepped in front of me and shaded me from the sun. Their arms were crossed. On the left, a tall woman with a distinct parrot beak and oversize eyes made a parrot-like squawk. The other woman had an owl head. Both took a step backward away from me as if I frightened them. I was pleased to see them back up because I found them downright freaky. The effect was too perfect to be masks or a trick.

The gorgeous redhead turned back to face me. She leaned toward me and said something I couldn't understand. She smelled wonderful, like walking down the perfume aisle in Redmond's department store — which I had done only once, by accident I mean. Her face was almost pixie-like. My heart began to beat a little harder.

Was I dead? Or maybe someone had slipped me an LSD sugar cube, because the world looked, well, so damned weird: those bird women that chirped; an impossibly beautiful woman wearing body tight clothes; a pair of four-armed people walked past juggling six rings each; and a man with impossibly strong legs who leaped sixty feet into the air and vanished well beyond the crowd. I looked again at the giant-sized dog with intelligent looking eyes next to me. Did the dog raise a single eyebrow?

The woman said something to the dog.

The dog said something to her in a language she understood but I didn't.

The language the woman and dog spoke resembled one of those rapid fire auctioneers in the south, but foreign sounding too, with a strangely musical quality and without my ability to understand a single word.

A shadow passed over me. Two huge birds? No wait. Those weren't birds, they were men with huge wings, one grey, the other bright green, in majestic flight. Furry but colorful men like monkeys with angel wings. Nothing like the flying monkeys in the Wizard of Oz though. More like real angels.

I should be dead, I remembered dying, I remembered that airliner crashing into me as I tried to run from it. So what was I doing sitting? And where was I sitting? And how could I be sitting at all?

The gorgeous woman leaned in and caught my attention again. She moved her mouth carefully and asked, "Who are you?"

Suddenly able to understand her, I smiled. "Wow," I said. "You are one really fine looking woman." And I was being honest. Her skin was flawless, her hair red and orange, and smooth, her eyes purple, a deep purplish blue. I couldn't take my eyes off her.

The parrot women spoke the same rat-tat-tat language I couldn't understand. I looked up at them and then at the redhead and then back at the dog. A real short haired, brown dog with deep brown eyes, seated on the ground and looking at me at eye level. Gazing at the dog eye to eye I realized its tail had started to wag.

More and more people passed by, beyond the edge of where I sat, creatures and humans of all sorts, of all smells, most good and some bad, and all making a wide range of sounds. "Am I in heaven or hell?" I asked. "Or maybe in limbo. If I was religious that is, or if I believed. Anyway, I tell you, I'm not into the afterlife. This is more like a cartoon, a surreal cartoon, maybe a Salvador Dali cartoon. Oh! Am I really in a set from that new Star Wars film?" I looked around. "Where's the camera?" I thought I was being funny but clearly I wasn't.

The two bird-headed women squawked something in unison, and then they turned as if choreographed, and walked off, their matched skirts swirling around multiple interior hoops, and their bird heads bobbing and tweeting at each other as if exchanging secrets. The effect was so perfect they couldn't have been wearing costumes.

The redhead stepped closer to the me and studied my face. She reached out and touched the side of my head. Her hand was much warmer than I expected, almost too hot, like she was running a fever.

"Your skin is too cool," she said.

I instinctively reached to pull her closer, but my hands felt unfamiliar. So instead I looked at them. They were different colors, one black the other woefully pale,

as were my wrists, one tan and one hairy and old looking. I was wearing black pants and a white shirt, and
my pants were tucked into what felt like stout boots. I
wiggled my toes inside my boots.

The dog opened its mouth again and said,
"There's no afterlife because there's no death. Even
intelligent dogs live forever."

I looked at the dog seated on its haunches eye to
eye with me. "You mean you're immortal?"

The woman sat down next to me. I saw the bench
rise up to meet her butt as she sat. I had no idea how a
bench could do that.

"Not exactly," she said. "Oh and my name's
Windy3."

"You smell really nice. Like a professional I once
smelled in a dance club, a new one down in Soho." I
looked away from her. Up close her eyes were almost
too big and almost too purple. "Or maybe I was that
concert outside Memphis. Or that woman that made
me get a tattoo of a lion on my ass when I was too
drunk and stoned to know better." I tried to think of a
woman like Windy3, someone from my past, but came
up empty.

The dog said, "The gods claim to be immortal,
but everyone else is simply not allowed to die." The dog
turned its head and looked back down the road. "I
smell snufflers."

Windy3 stood up quickly and muttered, "Oh no!"
She rubbed her hands together nervously. She looked
back down the road, turning her head from side to side
looking for something. "Too soon," she muttered.

The dog looked at her. "They're not after you are
they?"

She nodded her head weakly.

"What are snufflers?" I asked.

"No time," the dog said and nudged me in the ribs with its cold nose. "We should run."

Windy3 stood and looked sideways at the me. She seemed to hesitate, but then said, "Yes, really hurry."

I stood, but found myself still a little unsteady and still bent. I carefully stood up straight and took a hesitant step. All the people passing by made the roadway bounce and sway just enough to throw my balance into question. I frowned and said, "My left boot seems seriously too short. But, yes, I guess I can walk, maybe even run."

Windy3 took my hand and looked at me. "You have brown spots on your neck, that makes you seem positively primitive. Like a man who might have been born two-hundred years ago, back before all people could be perfect."

The dog nudged me forward with his moist nose making my back feel wet. At the edge of the road was a wide ramp that led to a tall set of double glass doors into the side of a skyscraper.

We started across that ramp. I looked over the edge and let out a startled shout. I jumped backward a step and bumped into Windy3's fevered body. "There's no safety rail!" I said a bit too loudly. The ramp was flat from side to side with no sign of anything like a rail to provide safety. I stepped cautiously forward again, but not too close, and bent to peer over the edge. Far below, disappearing from view were ribbons of hundreds of roads winding around and between dozens and dozens of high rises that punctuated the sky. All those roads were covered with hundreds of people and booths and the occasional long bus winding through the crowds. Ground level between the buildings appeared mostly deserted. And those buildings! I felt my mouth hang open. Each towering hi-rise looked different, both in color and design. One was bright green and shaped like a cork-screw. Another was pale yellow and shaped like a tall pencil but with bell shaped balconies jutting from all over like the buds of a tree. Yet another appeared to be constructed of jewels and sparkled as I moved my head. There must have been dozens of towering hi-rises ranging as far as I could see. "What happens to people that fall over the edge?" I asked. And then I thought I saw someone fall off a far distant road. A dot, really, but I was sure it could have been a person.

"If you die," Windy3 said and tugged my shirt to guide me toward the doors. "An Angel will come."

"Not real angels of course," the dog said walking ahead of us. "Machines that look like Angels."

"Doors won't open for me," Windy3 said. "I guess you'll die here."

The dog trotted ahead to the doors, which opened automatically. The dog held the doors open by standing between them. "It's always good to travel with a dog. Doors always open for me," the dog said.

Windy3 hesitated, and then pulled on my shirt and led me through an amazingly high and wide pair of glass doors. The doors were unusually thick, more than a yard, but clear glass not green. Once we were through, the dog followed us, and allowed the doors to wheeze heavily shut behind us. The lobby became dead quiet and was a bit too warm.

We had arrived in a high-ceiling lobby that curved away at the far end with elevator doors lining both walls. The air inside was dry and odorless. Wendy3 began walking down the long line of elevator doors looking for one to take. But to me, she looked worried and lost. Remarkably beautiful. I remembered my two different colored hands and imperfect face and wondered if I would ever stand a chance with a woman again.

I noticed a tall, thin man standing by an elevator door near the entrance. The carpet felt like real grass underfoot but it was deep blue. My legs were two different lengths so I hobbled back to talk to him.

The man looked imposing in his black-cloth western duster, but was otherwise just another human. No beak, no wings. "Hi," I said.

"You can see me?" the tall man asked with a genuine look of puzzlement on his face. He had one of those long faces like people I once knew. Like a man I once hitchhiked a ride home with, in his comfortable Cadillac. He had been a county judge who lectured me on the risks of hitchhiking.

The tall man's forehead was tattooed with a strange symbol like a crescent moon sideways with two stars above. A strange symbol that resembled the smile of a Cheshire cat.

I looked up at him "Of course I see you. Why do you ask? Are you supposed to be invisible?"

"I'm a ghost," the tall man said. "You're not supposed to be able to see me. And did you know you're talking Ancient English instead of Worldspeak?"

Windy3 walked up and asked me, "Who you talking to?"

I looked at her and realized I'd never told her my name. "Puppet," I said.

"What?" She ask and stared at me.

"My name's Puppet."

The tall ghost stretched out his hand to shake. "Glad to meet you Puppet," he said. "I'm Horace, an historian."

I shook his hand. "Glad to meet you Horace."

"No," Windy3 said, and her eyes moved around but it was clear she didn't see him. "Are you talking to a ghost?"

Horace nodded at Windy3 and said, "Ordinary people can't see or hear me."

The dog trotted over, sat and leaned against me but looked up at Horace. "I can see you," the dog said to Horace.

Windy3 squeaked a harshly surprised noise and stepped quickly backward. "Oh no, not so soon!"

A huge creature had appeared just beyond the glass. It resembled a giant mole but bigger than an elephant, with beady, red eyes and tentacles sprouting from both sides of its head and a huge nose like a vacuum-cleaner hugging the ground and pumping as if following a scent. It's tentacles created a terrible racket on the glass of the doors. Fluffy hairy eyebrows surrounded its tiny eyes, and thick white fur covered its body that shook and rippled as it worked its tentacles. Each tentacle was like an octopus except two tentacles that were thick ended, like a squid but with fingers formed into fists.

A second creature walked up next to it and its tentacles too began beating on the glass doubling that horrible racket. The glass began to crack.

Horace asked, "Who are the snufflers after?"

I pointed at Windy3 whose shoulders slumped making her look all the more helpless. I stepped closer to put my arm around her, but she took a step back. I let my arm drop. I remembered my first wife. I sighed.

Longer cracks had started to appear in the glass of the huge double doors, which seemed to encourage the snufflers. They began to beat on the glass even harder.

All those doors must be elevators, but I could see no buttons to call them. I began to tap my right foot nervously, the shorter of the two. "So that's a snuffler," I said. My eyes went wide when a third snuffler, larger than the first two, try to squeeze between them, it tentacles waving hard but not yet meeting the glass. "Is there another way out of here?"

Next to me, Windy3 said "Oh no."

Even though I was pleased to have met such a lovely woman, I was sad to think I was about to be killed again. But I realized I might have time to say good-bye first. I opened my mouth to speak, but I was drown out by terrible noise.

The snufflers had broken the glass up high. A thick chunk and then a larger chunk, fell inward with the solid sounds of heavy stones hitting the floor. I could feel the vibration through my feet as they settled. The third, much larger snuffler noticed the damage and began to beat harder and more furiously against the glass with its massive tentacles. I could hear them clearly through the large hole. One of them let out a high wailing sound that hurt my ears. Tentacles waved inside the lobby over my head. A cool wind blew through the hole and reminded me of a sea breeze, but I had no idea where the ocean might be.

The elevator door behind Horace opened silently and Horace stepped back into it casting his shadow out across the blue-grass floor. He stopped part-way in so he could hold the door open with his shoulder. "Care to join me?" He glanced at the wall inside the door. "I believe I am on an express elevator, all the way down."

"Hurry," I said, and grabbed Windy3 by her hot hand and pulled her toward the elevator. She was surprisingly light. She resisted my pull which caused me to stumble over a chunk of glass.

Tentacles grabbed her legs and, quicker than I could react, she was pulled upside down into the air. I still held onto her hand. "No!" I shouted. "Don't let go!" I clamped my other hand over hers for a better grip. I held hard, intending to not let go no matter what.

Her eyes were wide in panic. "Save me," she said. "Save me strange man. Only you can save me. Only you can risk your life to save me."

I held on tight, but the strength of the snufflers was too great. The snuffler made a buzzing sound, and Windy3 was pulled from my hands effortlessly, as if I was a mere child.

"No!" I shouted.

And then I felt Horace's grip on my belt as he pulled me onto the elevator.

The dog hurried onto the elevator last, as the elevator door shut. I heard the sound of large chunks of glass falling and heavy rumbling creature-steps. The other snufflers must have forced their way into the lobby apparently after us too. Loud pounding sounded outside the closed elevator door. The elevator vibrated with their movement.

"Oh no," I said. "It sounds like they're trying to break down the elevator door too."

A Rapid Descent

Something like magnetism grabbed my feet and ankles almost to my knees, and held them down firmly against the floor. The elevator fell and then sped faster and faster downward. I felt my hair —I actually had hair, lots of it!— float on either side of my head and then it all fell straight up as the elevator accelerated even more. For a few moments I felt as if I was hanging upside down.

I looked at Horace also hanging upside down his face partially blocked by his inverted coat. I noticed his hair hadn't moved at all. I asked him, "What were those monsters? And why couldn't Windy3 see you?"

Horace shook head sorrowfully. "She could neither see nor hear me nor see the things I touched or occupied. Like I said. I'm a ghost. She couldn't see the elevator even when you tried to pull her onto it."

My hands were still sweaty from holding her hot hands. "But why are you called a ghost?"

"Fifty years ago, rumors began about a second patchwork man appearing in the world. We historians wondered if other such patchwork men had appeared

29

before that and began to investigate. I suspect some of us might have found something that embarrassed the Immortals, because shortly after that all historians became invisible. Not really invisible, merely imperceptible to everyone else. And we could no longer communicate with each other. It has been a lonely fifty years. I lived as an observer who could not participate."

The elevator began to slow. My hair fell straight down again. The direction of down once again pointed at my feet. I had queasy feeling, like I had involuntarily done a back flip.

The dog jumped and said, "I don't like anything trapping my paws."

"That sounds sad, being a ghost, I mean," I said to Horace. I moved my feet. They were no longer stuck. "Man, those were terrible creatures. Windy3 told me that everyone was perfect. So why were they so ugly?"

The elevator eased to a smooth stop and the doors quietly opened into a dimly lit lobby with a low ceiling. The dog trotted out first, sniffed the air then turned and said, "You can come out."

I remembered Windy3, her kind smile and her soft, hot hands, and realized that I missed her. I had only known her for a few minutes, but I missed her anyway. I walked out and asked the dog, "What will the snufflers do to her?"

The dog stopped sniffing the air and said, "Take her back to the Council of Immortals would be my guess."

Horace stepped up next to me. "I can find no record of a Windy3 using my Soul. But one member of the Council of Immortals is named Windy2."

I was going to ask him about his soul, but noticed the room instead. It was dimly huge and wide with a low black ceiling dotted with thousands of pinpoint lights like stars twinkling above. The effect was so perfect that for a moment I thought that I was outside again under a nighttime sky. The floor was covered in something soft The room seemed to absorb sound.

Horace looked up too, his hands in the pockets of his long grey coat that almost reached the floor, and said, "Wow, zweeg."

"What?" I asked him.

"Sorry," he said. "There's no Ancient English word for 'fallen silent.' so I used the Ancient Dutch word instead. I wonder how I knew that? I guess my Soul knew that."

"Be quiet," the dog said. "I'm listening to the building talk."

"What's it saying?" I asked softly.

"The two smaller snufflers are stuck on the top floor. The only elevator they can fit into is a slow freight elevator. They act as if they are still after us despite the big one having already captured Windy3."

I looked around for an exit but saw only darkness and the glow of a long line of elevator doors.

Dog walked ahead, nose to the ground, and said, "The carpet smells like dirt, the dirt of many feet that have walked over it for many years. A thousand stories. No, a million stories."

I had no idea what kind of smell that could be, but I added, "In the city that never sleeps," from that Sinatra song my dad loved. I followed dog into darkness. I could hear myself limp and the long steps of Horace next to me.

As the dog approached the end of darkness, two opaque doors whooshed opened and grey daylight glimmered through. The dog paused in silhouette partway through the doors and wagged its tail. Horace and I hurried forward and outside into subdued daylight.

I breathed deeply in, glad to be outside again. "The air smells like grass after a lighting storm," I said.

Dog looked up at the sky and said, "I hear someone falling."

Soon we all heard it, a continuously varying scream. but not a scream. A woman falling appeared first as a dot, then grew rapidly, enlarging disturbingly fast, her arms and legs gyrating, her long hair flapping, her scream was clearly a perfectly enunciated yodel, more a Nordic yodel than a cowboy yodel —damn my dad's third girlfriend for teaching me that difference. Finally she appeared full sized and hit the ground hard, distorting her whole body, with a loud, hard crunching splat no more than a dozen steps distant. The most startling thing was the way her head seemed to explode like a melon. The yodel was cut off instantly.

A heavy drop of her blood spattered my face. "Jesus!" I said. "What the hell was that?" I wiped the blood off my cheek and looked at it on my finger tip. Or rather on someone else's finger tip that was mine.

"Might be a death addict," Horace said.

"Angel," the dog said and looked up again.

A large black box, shaped roughly like a toaster, deeply opaque-black underneath as if it was totally dark inside and empty, floated into view and descended at a stately pace, soon settled over and completely covered the dead woman. Atop the box was a large, quasi bowling pin but pure white with three abstract wings equally spaced around it. It rested there absolutely silent.

Horace said, "That's an Angel."

"I think it's a stretch to call that an angel," I said. I had barely finished speaking when the box rose up off the woman.

"Why didn't she resurrect on the upper road-way?" the dog asked.

"I didn't know we could do that," Horace said.

The woman stood there unharmed, even her clothing had been cleaned and repaired. She jumped up and down briskly and clapped her hands. She smiled and whooped with joy and seemed not to see us. Clapping her hands she ran passed us and through doors and into the lobby full of elevators up. As she passed by I thought her eyes looked glazed over.

I watched her as the doors closed behind her and then looked at my finger again. The blood was still there.

Introductions

"You ever died?" I asked Horace.

"Not yet. At least not that I remember."

"Trust me. It's not fun. And for most people it's permanent."

Dog walked quickly ahead of us and then turned and sat down on its haunches facing us. It opened its mouth and for one moment I had the image of the RCA Victor dog in my mind. It said, "You should all call me by my name, Gypsy. And as you can see, or should be able to see for yourselves, I'm a female."

I stepped forward, and as I crouched, I had a thought.This might real after all, and not an hallucination. I'd never taken acid myself, but the way others described their trips to me, none had ever been this elaborate or realistic or so well detailed.

On one knee, I faced a talking dog. A real live talking dog! "Pleased to meet you Gypsy." I began to lift my hand to shake, but didn't because I knew that was a second-nature dog trick from my previous life, so I let my hand drop. "My full name is Puppet Franc Zeno and I was born in Colorado and died in Kansas. Mom wanted the name Duke, but Dad insisted. He said that Puppet was his 'clown gut' speaking and that name would bring me good luck."

"Three names," Horace said. "Nobody these days as more than one, other than some families in the Southern Asian Ecosystems and there they sometimes have names as long as ten."

Gypsy asked, "When did you die?"

"1986," I said and stood again. My uneven legs started of ache too quickly while I had been crouched. "What year is it?"

Horace had walked over to stand next to Gypsy. "Years have adjusted several times over the centuries. Without those adjustments I would guess it is roughly 2280 or so."

The year 2280 made my head feel fuzzy. "So how does that work? I died in a plane crash in 1986 and wake up almost," I counted on my fingers, "300 hundred years later? Sitting on a bench, wherever that bench was."

"And in the body of an art man," Horace said and smiled.

Gypsy nudged me with her snout and said, "I know someone that might be able to help us with our snuffler problem, and you with your language problem."

"Who?" I asked.

"He is a porcupine man who lives off-Soul nearby. He raised my mother back before dogs could be intelligent. He is a kind but cautious man. In fact I should travel ahead to let him know you're coming." Gypsy turned and trotted ahead a few steps, then looked back and said, "Don't follow me too closely."

35

We began to follow Gypsy, far enough behind to not lose her. I noticed the side of the building next to me seemed to be slowly expanding. I wasn't sure if that was me or an illusion so I stepped close and felt it. Yes, it was definitely expanding. And then it paused and began to contract. It felt odd to me, the feel of cold, hard stone doing that. "It's expanding and contracting," I said.

Horace answered without slowing. "You wouldn't know of course, but the building is alive."

I hurried to catch up. "What do you mean?"

"All high-rises are alive. Not intelligent of course, but self building hives of self replicating micro-robots that keep a building growing slowly taller and taller. In another fifty years they'll probably double in height. Maybe high enough to require an artificial atmosphere. But more likely they'll become home to folks that don't need as much air." He thought for a moment. "The first self-growing buildings appeared about two-hundred years ago."

I looked up and in the distance saw another body falling. With all those high roads, I realized people falling must be a common sight. "Is that why we see so few people down here? Because folks fall from the roads overhead?"

"Not only people by accident and on purpose. Sometimes booths fall too, and once a long time ago I heard that a busman ran off the end of a road that hadn't finished growing. He took his hundred passengers over with him. And once in a heavy rain a dozen flying people flew hard into a building and fell. I'm sure there are more examples."

We rounded a bend in the road and came upon a smaller building between us and the next high rise. The building wasn't square, instead it was shaped like a watermelon with its bottom end chopped off so it could be stood upright on the ground. It couldn't have been more then two or three stories tall and was covered in hundreds of tiny round windows, like portholes. Around all the windows grew a profusion of thick leaved green ivy with a red tint.

Gypsy stopped and turned. "Wait here, while I prepare him for your visit," she said. She turned and trotted ahead and entered that odd looking building.

"About eighty years ago," Horace said. "There was a bad earthquake and several of the roads collapsed. You should have seen it. Thousands of Angels. It was really a sight to remember."

I tried to picture that but couldn't. "You know," I said. "I just remembered, I was once warned that I might die and wake up in the future."

"We have time," Horace said. "Tell me about it."

"It had been sooth sayer, a Russian woman. By a campfire on a beach," I said. "There was music playing, banjos and guitars and drums. I remember how she hurried away from me, let go of my hand and fled, afraid after she saw my future. Something about lightening and thunder and many people dying. That had been a weird prediction and one I still don't understand."

Quills And A Book

A loud bark from the building caught our attention. Gypsy stood in the open doorway and called loudly enough for us to hear, "He's happy to have you join him."

Gypsy was already seated on her haunches when we entered. She faced one of the strangest men I've ever seen. The man behind a low counter was black, I don't mean dark brown, but jet black as if drawn with India ink or born from a shadow. Massive and strong, the backs of his arms and the visible part of his back were covered with long black quills, thorn sharp and at least an arm's length long. His shape and size reminded me of a scary cartoon man. I stepped up to the counter and was surprised to discover that the whites of the man's eyes were black too, and there was about him an odor of chlorine.

Gypsy said, "Greeleech, meet Puppet."

I reached out my hand to shake. I watched a huge black hand that felt like a thick leather (but too warm) boxing glove swallow mine. "Man," I said. "You're really black."

"I wasn't born big and black," Greeleech said. His voice was deep and mellow. "I was a pasty Irish lad back then, at least I think I was Irish. But look at you, a man born out of time," He gave my hand a gentle squeeze and released it. Greeleech looked around. "One person. You said there'd be two." He looked at Gypsy. "You better not have brought me a ghost."

I turned and waved Horace over. "Shake his hand," I said. "He can't see you but maybe he can feel you."

Horace shrugged and extended his hand.

When their hands met, Greeleech stood straight with a start, and his quills flared so violently that I almost expected them to fire at me.

Greeleech asked Horace, "Are you a ghost that just appeared?"

"Pleased to meet you," Horace said.

Gypsy said. "Meet Horace. He's a historian."

"A historian? Really? Do you think he'd be interested in the back room?"

"Definitely," Gypsy said.

Horace looked at Gypsy. "What's in the back room?"

"Books," Greeleech said. "Thousands of preserved antique books. All of them hundreds of years old."

Horace's eyes opened wide. "Books? Real books."

"Better take a dry pad," Greeleech said. "Don't want him to drool on the books." He chuckled with a booming deep but happy sound.

"Follow me," Gypsy said and led Horace off in the direction of a large arched doorway hung with a hippie style beaded curtain in a red and blue striped design, like my juggling balls hundreds of years ago.

Greeleech leaned forward to gaze at me. "Gypsy told me you were being chased by snufflers."

I nodded.

"That's bad," Greeleech said with a heavy nod of his head. "Really bad. As I heard it, the only people with such low respect for others are the Counsel of Immortals. They're the only ones that play with snufflers and smellbats. Ugly creatures."

"Yeah," I said. "But can you help?"

"Of course," Greeleech said and spread his arms wide with a broad smile.

I was startled, but couldn't put my finger on what was wrong, then realize his teeth and tongue were black too.

Greeleech became serious and leaned forward toward me and asked, "You want to speak and understand our modern language? It is more succinct and universal then Ancient English. And people from other ecosystems may not be able to understand your English."

"Sure," I said. "Why not?"

"And give you a defense for your quest."

"What quest?"

"A quest for love. What other kind of quest is there?" Greeleech plucked two quills from his left arm and threw them with quick flicks of his wrists, too fast for me to even flinch out of the way. One stuck into my arm. I winced expecting pain but there was none. The other stuck into the top of my head, significantly to the left of center.

The quill in my arm pumped a glowing green liquid into my skin. Once the quill was empty it dropped off and left no mark. I felt the other quill fall off of my head. On the floor, both quills dissolved to bubbles. I nudged the bubbles with my toe but felt nothing, it was like nudging air. Behind me I heard something like hail hitting the building. I walked over to one of the lower round windows and looked out. A large bat hit the window with a loud thunk. Its nose was a triangular suction cup stuck to the window. Inside the triangle were sharp teeth that kept moving and made a scratching sound on the glass.

Greeleech looked up. "Smellbats. Always watch out for their teeth, they can etch glass. But don't worry, that's self-healing glass, and the ivy is poisonous to them. I gave you control over your scent. Think of how you want to smell and you're scent will change to match your desire."

"Old lady blue," I said. "Like my aunt Latki had."

The striped beads of the doorway rattled and Gypsy came thundering out. She skidded to a stop next to me. "I thought something had happened to you," she said. "Your scent suddenly vanished."

I looked back at the window and saw hundreds of smellbats flying off, most of them wobbling as if actually a bit poisoned. Almost all fell out of the sky to lay still on the ground. Their death pleased me. At least I thought they had been a threat. But here inside and safe, I was no longer certain how pleased I should be. I remembered how beneficial bats could be. Eating insects that would otherwise harm us or our crops.

Horace walked out carrying a book. He appeared oblivious to the fact that anything had happened. "I knew it existed," he said. "But all records of it have been erased from my Soul."

"What is it?" I asked.

"Moby Dick."

I smiled. "At last something I recognize. Queequeg was convinced he would die so he carved his own coffin. But he was the only survivor and survived only because he could use his coffin as a raft."

"Maybe that's why we've forgotten so much?"

"Because they're stories of death?"

Horace hugged the book to his chest as if it were a treasure. "No. Because the past has no bearing on the present."

I laughed. "I'm surprised to hear a historian say that. Most historians I ever knew said we couldn't understand the present with out first understanding the past."

From behind me, Greeleech said something to me that sounded like a machine gun firing vowels and consonants at a rapid rat-tat-tat, sing song rate.

I asked, "What'd you say?"

"How about that," Gypsy said. "You're speaking Worldtalk."

I laughed. "You're trying to pull the wool over my eyes. I'm talking the same way I was talking a few minutes ago. Nothing's changed."

"There," Greeleech said. "You'll be able to talk to most folks. It's the best I could do considering you don't have Soul in your brain. So I gave you the next best thing. A pseudo-Soul on the outside of your head."

"What do you mean a soul?"

Greeleech leaned on his counter and his bulk caused it to groan in protest. "You have to be resurrected with one and you weren't. When you outside Soul matures you can use it to communicate mentally."

Horace looked at my head, "You don't have Soul?"

"There's a man you need to see. He'll be able to explain better," Greeleech said. "He's the guardian of the bones at End Station on the River East." He glanced over at Gypsy. "I transferred a transit map into your Soul."

Gypsy became silent for a moment and then said, "We should hurry, there's only four transports a day."

"What kinds of bones is he guarding?" I asked Greeleech. "And why do I have to go?"

"Trust me," Greeleech said and extended his hand to shake. "It's critical you see them."

I leaned across the counter. "Thanks, Greeleech," I said. "I mean it."

Greeleech looked at me with a hard expression. "Don't let anything happen to these people because of your quest."

I hesitated, uncertain I could protect anyone in this new world. "I won't."

"I sense you're a myth in the making," Greeleech said, but let it hang without explanation.

Light streamed into the building. Gypsy stood in the open doorway. "We need to hurry," she said.

Horace waved the book at Greeleech and said, "I will protect your book at all costs."

"Farewell ghost," Greeleech said and then looked at me, "You too, the man of many men."

I let the door swing shut behind me and wondered what sort of myth or symbol I might be. Nothing came to me so I shrugged and followed the others out into that shadowed daylight.

Lesson In Corn

Every one of smellbats that had fallen to the ground were gone. The must have been only stunned and flown off. "Strange," I said.

Gypsy said to us, "The entrance to transport is in the lobby of highrise after the next highrise."

Horace dropped the book he'd been given into an internal pocket of his long coat, and patted it as if it were an old friend. His coat was black again. The smile on his face reminded me of the smile of a proud father.

"I like the way your coat changes colors," I said.

"Yes it turns gray in the dark and black in daylight. Not a wide range of colors."

His modest answer surprised me. "In my day I would have given anything for a coat that changed colors."

He nodded ahead. "We should get going."

The three of us set off for the terminus building that turned out to be much further away than I expected. My uneven boots no longer felt uncomfortable, but I knew I would have sore feet tomorrow. We passed several food stalls. One had no customers and no one behind the counter. Another was surrounded by a group of people wearing brightly colored clothes with outrageously tall hats. That stall appeared to be selling ice cream. The sequence of aromas reminded me that I was hungry. "How do I buy food from one of those stalls?" I asked Horace.

Horace answered, without pausing his stride, "Most food is free. Sometime you have to barter."

"Really?"

"Of course," Horace said and nodded at a booth we were approaching. "Ask for what you want."

I hurried forward at a crisp hobble and found a woman behind the counter with a pincer instead of a left hand. At first I thought it was a plastic pincer, but realized that was an assumption from my previous life. Behind her on a grill were several ears of corn with the husks already removed. I could smell the hickory coals and remembered the one time my dad tried to barbecue. He had grilled corn too —mostly burned, but still good with butter.

"May I have one?" I asked as politely as I could muster. She seemed totally normal except for that pincer. Her short cut hair combed forward almost covered her eyes. Her polka dot dress was hard to look at because the dots seemed to be moving slowly around. I blinked and they stopped moving, then turned into squares that danced. Her butcher-style high topped apron had an image of a corn stalk sewn to it.

"A whole one?"

"Yes, please," I said. "I'm really hungry."

The woman shrugged, turned briskly and pulled a cob off the grill using her pincer and turned back to face me with a flourish and handed me the cob. "Bred to be easy to digest and with a full day's nourishment," she said. "And with lime-butter flavor bred in."

Other than two indentations from the pincers, the corn looked delicious. It was quite warm but not too hot to hold. I could smell the butter. "Do I owe you anything?"

The woman looked at me as like I had spouted nonsense. "I did you no favor. You only owe me if I do you a favor." She turned partway to tend her corn, but thought better of it and turned back to face me again. "Next time you get corn from someone, let them know Mollycorn makes the best corn." Her smile was ambiguous so I couldn't tell if she was serious or not.

I hurried and caught up with the others. I used my teeth to strip a few rows of kernels off. But under those kernels were more kernels. "You mean the kernels extend all the way through?"

"No, there's a thin cob in the middle," Horace said.

I finished my corn and felt well filled and satisfied. I broke the cobb into three parts and juggle them as we walked. "Is everything free?"

Horace glanced sideways at me. "Depends what you mean," he grinned, then looked ahead again. "All the people are free except for the ability to die. There is no governance anymore, or what I think government might have been, not like you knew when you first lived. Instead everything is intelligent and takes care of us. Our clothing, for example," he plucked his coat. "It's aware of itself and repairs any rips or wear and repels dirt and stains. If you want to change your style of dress, find someone that loves to make clothing. Some people make clothes with special properties, like resisting fire or being totally waterproof. Sometimes you have a talent of your own or possess something they need and ask for that in return. Really fair."

My new arms weren't used to juggling and were growing tired. "I'm looking for someplace to toss away these cobs," I said, as we neared the next building. I stopped juggling and covered my mouth to suppress a belch.

"Throw the pieces on the street," Horace said.

Uncertain if I should, I hesitated and then reluctantly tossed the three cob pieces to one side. As I watched, three holes in the street opened, swallowed each cob piece, and closed again. I almost expected the street to burp like I had.

"Self cleaning streets," Horace said.

"Why doesn't it swallow our feet?" I asked, but Horace ignored me.

Ah, I thought as I remembered. The vanishing, dead smellbats. I guess they didn't fly away after all.

Horace looked at something directly in front of his eyes and said, "Interesting. No make that amazing! The history message board is back again, and there are new shared messages. I never thought I'd see this day again." He choked up, then cleared his throat. "How wonderful. Many of the historians that had become ghosts are back."

Bite Sized

The door under the Terminus Elevator sign had a small hand-written note attached to it. In fancy cursive, it read, "Warning, boarding platform flooded."

"What do we do?" I asked.

"Go down and see," Horace said. "If the elevator floods, we can just come back up."

That seemed risky to me. I was about to suggest he go down first and check it out, but the door opened and I was in front, so I was gently herded in.

The elevator stopped and the door's opened. I felt myself flinch. But instead of water rushing in to drown us, a path led out and through the center of what looked like a tunnel carved out of brown water. I exhaled and realized I had been holding my breath.

Horace stepped out first and reached with his long hand and poked the wall. The wall rippled there but his finger came away dry. "How about that," he said and looked at me waiting inside the elevator door. "I'd say we're safe."

I walked out next, followed by Gypsy.

I looked around. The tunnel appeared to run into the dim distance. "What is it? Some kind of force field?"

Horace gazed in front of his eyes, then his vision seemed to clear and he looked at me. "The only thing I've been able to find is a reference to a microscopically thin new-spider silk with a weave too small to let air out or water in."

Gypsy slipped past us and announced, "The last transport arrives in a few minutes. We'd better hurry." She trotted ahead to lead the way.

At the end of the walk stairs led down and to the left. We descended into an even larger tube and a short platform that was comfortably wide. Floating in the air above the platform, with no visible means of support, glowing numbers counted down from two minutes. "Soon," Gypsy said.

Horace glanced at the clock and added, "Less than a minute." His eyes went wide as he noticed something.

I looked up and felt an involuntary start as my body jerked. A huge fish, its mouth beginning to open, layers and layers of pointed white teeth completely surrounding the mouth. On either side of its head were the deep black eyes of a simple brute. It approached and grew larger fast. Gypsy rubbed my leg as she moved backward away from the fish.

The fish's teeth met the end of the tunnel and tore through the thin fabric holding the water at bay. A hard spray hit me in my chest quickly soaking me with icy water. I rubbed water from my face and tasted salt water. I noticed that the stairs up and out were between me and the fish. The fish's mouth opened wider and the tube under the platform began to fill with water.

I looked sideways at Horace and said, "I don't want to be eaten."

Horace didn't look at me but stood transfixed by the approaching teeth. His legs were shaking. He squeaked, "I never want to die again."

Former Busman

That huge fish mouth with its terrifying teeth tearing fabric, finally withdrew its teeth and opened its mouth wide enough to form a perfect seal with the cylinder of fabric. The rush of water ceased and gurgled away under the boarding platform. I wiped chilly saltwater off my hair and face, and held my shirt away from my chest to shake it somewhat dry.

Instead of a tongue, the fish had stairs inside its mouth. Stairs embed with lights and a glow from the top of the mouth. Then the stairs began to move. The stairs became an escalator running down into the belly of the fish.

Horace announced with a deep wet cough that seemed to echo off the fabric-held water, "The transport has arrived."

Gypsy shook herself hard to dispel water from her coat. Her ears flap loudly and her shaking sprinkled me wet again.

Horace led the way down. Gypsy next and I followed last. The bottom opened into a comfortable cabin with high curved ceilings covered in a dark rib-like wood. A dry warm breeze helped dry my clothes. The walls were lined with large windows, with a view of murky water. Comfortable looking seats and pillows ranged down both side of a central aisle. What had first been a fish oil smell gave way to the soft aroma of freshly oiled teak. The windows were wrapped in stout bronze fitting that were brightly polished. Outside through the windows I saw only brown water until a small silver fish swam near enough to be seen. I plopped into a seat and felt is adjust to fit me perfectly. A warm breeze seemed to pass right through the seat and helped finish drying me out completely. What started out terrifying, transformed into the lap of luxury. Kind of like stumbling out of a terrible storm into the friendly tavern of a fancy hotel. "Ah Monterey," I whispered.

"Please be seated," spoke a mellow voice. "I will be departing soon."

"Who are you?" I asked.

"Bonbon," said the voice. "I used to be a busman and carried people all over the city. But I went off the end of an incomplete road one too many times. The horrible pain my passengers felt when we hit the ground, ah, well, after a while it became too much to bear."

"You were a bus?" I asked.

"A bus with feet technically. But when this underwater terminal opened, me and some other busmen decided to become underwater transport instead. And nobody has died yet."

"I've seen an Angel," I said. "And it was too small to make such a large fish."

Bonbon laughed. "The fish is a bio-machine, silly. I run it from my home. But, you're perfectly safe, I assure you."

I wasn't at all certain how safe a robot fish could be, but it felt solid enough. Still, I gripped the arm rests a bit too hard. I breathed in and tried to relax.

Horace next to me said, "Mind if I sit by you?"

I looked up at him and finally notice how young he looked. "Please friend," I said.

Horace sat, as the fish named Bonbon began to move. A smooth motion, much like a train pulling out from a station, but with more acceleration that pushed me back into my seat. Outside the windows, bits of undersea plants began to drift by, mostly kelp and other bits of seaweed, all moving past faster and faster. A man with a fish-shaped head swam up to the window and held onto the glass using suckers on his hands and fingers. His eyes were on either side of his head so he had to turn body sideways to look inside

"What's that?" I asked and touched the glass. I was startled to feel the glass deform soft under my finger. I jerked my hand away.

"I don't know," Horace said. "I've never seen anything like that before."

I leaned closer to the glass and looked the fish-man over. "His arms look really strong."

And then the fish-man released his grip and vanished. Bubbles rose beyond the windows and were quickly swept away.

"You'll excuse me if I say so," I said to Horace. "But you look awfully young to be a historian.

"I've always wondered about that myself," Horace said and leaned back into his seat. "I decided to be young when I was first resurrected. But I don't remember how old I was before that."

"I asked my Angel," Bonbon said. "But my Angel said he wasn't allowed to tell me. Some new rule."

Bonbon, or rather the fish that was controlled by him, turned and slowed, and then drew to a smooth stop.

Horace stood and said, "I believe we've arrived."

I looked back and noticed Gypsy curled up on a large pillow, comfortably taking a nap. The escalator ran uphill.

We said our good-byes to Bonbon and exited the large fish to another underwater platform. A short staircase led up through a wide, hard glass tube that ended on the surface on a solid looking wooden floating-dock that overlooked a remarkably wide, brown river. The day was still warm and insects buzzed and fluttered almost unseen all around us. A large white bird with a long, bent neck looked at us as we emerged. It took flight and flew majestically away, its wide wings flapping slowly as it soared into the distance.

Gypsy, next to me, also watched the bird. "An original great egret, I believe," she said.

I watched the bird disappear behind a distant row of trees.

Gypsy added, "I thought they were extinct because of the red-back egrets that where created last decade. A superior bird that drove the original into extinction."

I asked, "Have many of the original animals become extinct?"

Horace stepped up on the other side of me. "People keep bringing them back. They may not be able to compete, but they will never disappear."

I asked, "Do they bring back dinosaurs and the dodo too?"

"Not in this ecosystem," Horace said and sniffed the air. "I've heard they brought back some dinosaurs in the Southern African Ecosystem using some new DNA system."

The sound of a rattlesnake reminded me of the California desert. I looked at Horace who appeared oblivious to the sound.

Big Snakes

Gypsy sniffed the air and growled a low cautious growl.

Horace put his hand on my shoulder, heavy enough to slow me, and pointed inland.

Rising slowly behind the bushes lining the shore was a huge, really huge, bright red snake's head with a matching red flickering tongue. And somewhere behind that snake head was the sound of a rattle.

I spoke first, "It's a rattlesnake. A giant red rattlesnake?"

The snake withdrew its tongue and said, "Good gosh no! That rattling sound is my fourth wife practicing with maracas." His head rotated around to face inland. "Honey, please stop your practicing. We have guests." The snake had an average midwestern sounding man's voice, it didn't sound snake-like at all.

Gypsy growled softly, then looked up at me and said, "I don't trust snakes."

Horace was already walking up toward the line of bushes. I glanced at Gypsy and her tail was down and she looked genuinely unhappy.

I turned and began to follow Horace. Gypsy followed me a few paces behind.

Off to my right the city was small and distant. I hadn't realized that the fish transport had swum so far and so fast.

Bushes along the shore were formed into a complex topiary of twisted worms. At first that tangle was too dense to pass through, but as we approached, the plants grew down as if by magic to form a gap that was precisely rectangular. I followed Horace through the gap. The red snake had withdrawn onto the porch of a run-down house, with over-hanging eves reminiscent of old shacks I had once seen in the deep south. There was even moss growing between the irregular wooden shingles.

Arms and hands had appeared sprouting from the snake's side below his head. And he held one hand out in greeting.

Horace shook that hand.

The snake asked him, "That dog isn't going to chase us or bite us is it?"

Horace looked back at Gypsy then turned back to the snake. "No, she's an intelligent dog."

I stepped up next to face Horace. The snake looked me over.

"Say," the snake said. "I've seen people like you before. Patchwork art people I mean." He sounded sad. "Travelers like you."

"Really?" Horace said. "What happened to them?"

The snake half-laughed a chuckle which caused his forked tongue to flick out. "That was years ago you have to understand. The first was a century ago, the latest was fifty years ago. Say! You want to see them?"

Gypsy had finally approached close. "Did you kill them?" she asked.

"Us? No." The snake shook his head. "We're herbivores. Our digestion is a mammal's digestive tract and we have hearts." He chuckled again. "Being cold blooded seemed too difficult. So we opted to be warm blooded snakes."

"Like me," Gypsy said. "I can only eat plant protein. I never eat meat. Although I do love the occasional salmon."

The snake seemed to relax. It's coil appeared to become less compact and tense.

I said, "My name's Puppet. Meet Horace, and the dog is Gypsy."

"I must seem terribly rude to you. But we get guests so rarely. I'm George."

"Hi George," I said.

Horace said, "So tell us about those earlier travelers."

"Better you should see for yourselves," George said. "You'll never believe without seeing first hand."

"Lead on," I said, but whispered to Horace, "I have a bad feeling about this."

The snake George folded its arms and hand back into slits along its side and then slowly slithered off the porch and around the side of the building.

I trotted ahead to walk alongside George's head as the others waited for the end of the tail to appear. "Are you mostly a machine?"

"Nope," when he was moving he lisped a bit like a cartoon snake. "100% an organic body."

That made no sense to me. He was so big, easily five times bigger than the Angel I had seen. "How long have been a snake?" I asked.

"Only eighty years. Twenty years after that first poor patchwork man came back. That's when I met the five sisters and they convinced me to become a snake like them. Sex games you see."

The path beside the old house led up a low hill to a stone structure with a cross on its roof. I recognized it at once as a large sepulcher. It was squat and wide with two stone steps leading up into a dark interior. George slithered up the worn steps first followed by the others. I waited and entered last. Two stone platforms stood, one on either side, On top of each platform lay the skeleton of a man. The one on the right still wore thin bits of clothing. The one on the left was nothing but white bones.

George had slithered behind the platforms, where he curled up higher than us, and nodded at the bare skeleton on my left. "He was the first one. I was a man back then and he arrived by himself. He told me he was on a quest to the head of the river to kill the Immortals. He was a patchwork man too," He nodded at me. "He was tall and muscular and looked strong enough to pull it off. We made love that night and he departed the next morning in the same boat he had arrived in, a canoe loaded with supplies. He looked so majestic paddling up river, the sun off to his left making his blond hair shine. What a magnificent man. What a sensitive and noble man. A week later he came floating back, face down on the river, so I fished him out and laid him on the ground and waited for an Angel to resurrect him. But no Angel arrived and after a few days he began to stink, so I moved him inside."

I looked at the skeleton and asked, "Why didn't an Angel come?"

George said to Horace, "Pick up the skull and shake it."

Horace did so. The skull was silent.

George said, "No rattle. Never was. That patch-work man had no Soul in his head."

Horace looked back at my head.

I frowned. "What do you mean?"

Horace said, "When you are first resurrected, you are told you have a Soul in you brain and from then on you can be resurrected without losing your memory. Of course none of us can remember what happened before that. You can remember the past, though, and that makes you important."

George said, "I thought I had converted that man into a mortal with my unnatural homosexual behavior. So I became a heterosexual. But I was wrong." He pointed at the other skeleton. "He arrived alone as well. But he had no idea were he wanted to go, so he settled in that house you first saw. He eventually cut himself while chopping wood and bled to death. Again, no Angel came to resurrect him. And again there was no soul in his brain. And I never touched him!"

Horace walked over and put his hand on my shoulder. "Sorry, but it seems you may be mortal after all."

I noticed that everyone was looking at me. "Well ain't that a fine kettle of fish," I said.

Horace looked confused. "What fish?"

"That's an old expression. It means," I said. "I suspected that was too much to hope for."

But then I frowned. "What's so important about a Soul? Why does a Soul have to do with resurrection?"

"I know the answer to that," George said and slithered forward. "In addition to giving us instant accesses to all our friends, and allowing us to communicate with anyone anywhere, the Soul also records everything we think and feel and experience. So when we die, an Angel can rebuild our body and brain and repopulate the brain with all the memories, both physical and mental, that preceded death. That way we are resurrected with all our memories intact, including the memory of how we last died."

Horace said, "You speak as if you have died at least once."

"Yes," George said. "That's how I became a snake." He brought more of his body under himself and raised a bit so he could unfold his arms. Then he began to gesture as he talked. "It was the five sisters, you see. They had a suicide pact so they could become snakes. They had all died several times before and knew the secret. Turns out when you are resurrected, the Angel has a conversation with your soul, and if you last desire was to be resurrected as something else, they comply. I remember those five Angles rise all at once off the those five sisters and finding five huge snakes in their place. They talked me into letting them kill me so I could become a snake too." He bowed. "My guilt convinced me. The way I caused that first man to die, you see. So I have become the red snake you see humbly coiled before you."

Tumbled Out

George gave us a tour of the property. It must once have been a cemetery because the dirt appeared littered with broken grave stones. I noticed a, "d 19" on one chunk of stone and presumed it meant a person had died in my century. The ground was lumpy but the central path smooth and that was where George slithered. I walked on the smooth part too because the rough ground made my uneven legs ache.

Horace wandered alongside looking for intact stones but found none.

"All the bodies are gone," George said. "Taken I suspect to create patchwork people like you. Art people I mean, but none of them can animate like you did."

"The two skeletons and that's it," I said and realized the smell of dirt felt normal and reminded me of the dirt I once smelled in Kansas.

"Yes," George said. "Only those two."

"And one every fifty years," I said. "As if some event is being celebrated. Like the centennial of a battle, or the bicentennial of a country's founding."

We crested the hill and beyond lay a large area of sand with a bowl shaped depression in its center. Five different colored snakes lay woven together in the depression. All five snakes held instruments and were playing music together. To my ear the music sounded complex and a bit atonal, but Horace said, "What a lovely simple dance tune."

The music stopped and the five snakes all turned their heads to watch us walk down hill toward them. The yellow snake appeared to be the leader because she slithered out of the weave carrying maracas and headed uphill to meet us. "My first wife Ginger," George said.

George and Ginger met and slithered themselves around each other, stopping high over the heads of us two humans, the kissed and wrapped their forked tongues together, and embraced with their arms. Despite appearing to be real snakes, their faces were clearly soft, thus allowing a more human-like kiss.

I noticed Gypsy, far off to one side. She sat back on her haunches and watched. I thought I might want to walk over and ask her what her impressions might be. But before I could, I felt myself lifted up into the air and moved along on my back under a flat blue sky without a cloud to be seen. I had no idea what had happened, but was more fascinated than afraid.

"What a wonderful mix," I heard one voice say.

"Maybe he'll come back as a checkered snake," said a second voice quite close.

I heard Gypsy barking far away. A shout of, "Hey, no, stop!" from somewhere far behind me.

Suddenly I felt myself drop slowly and saw myself surrounded by snakes of different colors. I landed suddenly tumbling like a rag in a dryer. I smelled the acrid oder of what might have been snake sweat but didn't understand how snakes could sweat. The skin of the snakes were softly moist and textured so I was entertained by the feeling of them slipping past for a while, but then noticed I was being squeezed on all sides. I tried to push the snakes away but my arms were pinned. I felt my chest compressed and all at once found it hard to breathe. Much too hard to breathe. I heard, "A plaid snake." I started to lose consciousness.

A Plea For Help

I awoke and my chest hurt like hell. I tried to breathe in and that minor effort hurt worse. I heard myself wheeze.

I had been laid out on my back on a rock hard surface, and my butt and back were ice cold from lying on stone. I fluttered my eyes open. I was in the mausoleum again. I sat up and felt dizzy for a moment, and then I focused and saw I was lying on one of the two pedestals. It still hurt to breathe but not as bad as it did a minute ago. I pushed around on my chest with my hands and it ached but didn't hurt so I was certain I hadn't broken any ribs. Outside I could see the sun was orange and rising. For some reason my shoulders ached too.

The first skeleton was still on the platform beside me. Curious, I looked over the edge of my platform. Someone had dumped the second skeleton on the ground. I swung my legs over the edge and slipped off to stand, careful to not break any of any of the old bones on the ground. I brushed myself off and muttered, "What the hell happened?"

I piled the second skeleton back on the table was puzzling out how to reassemble it when I heard someone come in.

"You're alive!" It was Horace's voice. "Good morning. You stopped moving and wouldn't wake up so we assumed you would die."

"Have you forgotten how to revive people that have passed out?"

"What do you mean?"

"Oh that's right," I said. "You have Angels that do that. Did you say it was morning? Was I out all night?"

"Since before sunset," Horace said. He looked at the partially replaced skeleton on the platform. "Why are you putting it back? Do you do it because people used to honor their dead."

"No," I said a bit louder than I intended, and remembered that Native American woman I had met at the Grand Canyon. A relative of her's was one of the 38 Sioux men hanged in Mankato, Minnesota. The largest mass hanging in American history. She had suspected one of them might be her great grandfather. "You have it wrong," I said to Horace. "We never honored the dead. We tried to not forget the dead. That's entirely different."

Gypsy came in next and ran over to me and started sniffing me and wagging her tail at a furious rate. "You didn't die."

"No, but everyone thought I did." I started moving the leg bones into what seemed the right order based on the other skeleton.

George poked his large snake head through the door and said, "We have another visitor. Oh! You're alive."

"Who is it?" I asked.

"A man who says his brother was taken by fish."

I followed the others out of the mausoleum. I hurried the best I could with my aching body to see the visitor.

Ginger slithered up next to me. "Sorry," she said. "How were my sisters to know that you were the only man on the planet that could die?"

I stopped to talk to her and she stopped too. "You could have asked," I said and realized I was being rude. "You're right of course. They couldn't have known. But they sure can squeeze hard." I pulled up my shirt —not as high a I wanted because my arms and shoulders ached — so she could see my bruises.

"Sorry," she said again. "Those look really bad, but less bad on your dark patches."

Horace was talking to a man on a path well inland from the river. To me, the man looked like someone in his 40's, around my own age, or the age of the original me. He wore heavy boots, shorts and the kind of shirt that made him look like an old fashioned explorer.

Horace waved at me to come closer.

Gypsy was sniffing the stranger. The snakes looked the stranger over from well above him. I arrived next. I was out of breath. My chest still hurt, and I was thirsty.

Horace said, "Meet Ivan. His brother Christian was taken by a fish-man."

"I saw a fish-man recently," I said and winced. "He had suction cups on his fingers. They were stuck to the outside of those window of that big fish transport we took."

Ivan said, "My brother was taken by them. I believe they kept drowning him until he agreed to be one of them. He walked out of the river once, I believe to escape back to me. I recognized him by the blue bandana around his wrist. But several of the fish-men," he covered his mouth and sniffled in. "Rushed out of the water and pulled him back in."

"Why didn't he resurrect as a bear or a bull or something strong enough to escape?" Gypsy asked.

Ivan shook his head. "While I waited for him to try to get out again, I saw a elephant, a moose, an alligator, and a centaur all try to escape. But a dozen or more fish-men pulled them back in."

"Sounds to me like someone needs saving," I didn't realize I'd said it aloud until everyone looked at me. I suddenly wanted to add tomorrow so my bruises could begin to heal first, but I didn't.

"Good idea," George said and slithered off. "I'll tell the girls to get ready for a picnic and adventure."

Fish Fight

The river looked calm as we emerged from the bordering bushes. Not a ripple, not a hint of anything below the water's surface. All the snakes came along with a sense of adventure. So our patch of dirt above the sand was crowded.

I said to Ivan, "Please try to call your brother out of the water."

Horace stepped back toward the bushes and said, "I sense an historic moment. I'm setting my Soul's vision to stream out to the history folks live as it happens."

Ivan nodded at me, and then walked past Gypsy out onto the sand. He paused halfway to the water and called out, "Christian! If you can hear me Christian. Please come back to me." He glanced back at us. "I brought help. I brought help to save you Christian."

Nothing happened for a while. Horace stood silently and watched, surrounded by snakes. Across the river I heard two crows in a cawing argument. I found the scene relaxing. Then I saw ripples form on the water and a fish-man's head lifted from the river's surface.

Ivan took a step forward. "Christian? Is that you?"

The fish man stood up and was only waist deep as he began to walk out. A blue bandana was tied around his wrist.

"It's his bandana," Ivan said. "He always wore that when we hiked."

The bandana was limp and wet. Ivan reminded me of that rubber suit in the, "Creature From The Black Lagoon." A really old movie.

"Christian!" Ivan shouted and rushed forward toward his brother.

Another ripple formed and another fish-man emerged and followed Christian out of the water. The second fish-man was larger and looked much stronger than Christian. They were moving in slow motion because of the water.

"Watch out," I called.

More ripples formed and six more fish heads broke the surface.

The snakes made a racket as they turned and slithered away from the river, back through the sur-rounding bushes.

Even though I knew the plan, I had the sinking feeling I was being abandoned.

Ivan had reached his brother and tried to pull him away from the river. The second fish-man had already almost caught up with them.

The six other fish-men rose from the water and began to wade out.

"Hey," I yelled. I rushed forward.

It was hard to run through deep sand, but I got to Ivan and tried to pull the hostile fish-man off him but my hands slipped, as if the fish-man's skin was oiled. I tried to use my fingernails to hold a grip, but the arm was too slick. The fish-man let go of Ivan and use his suckers to grab onto me. I was almost pulled over. I used my free hand to punch the fish-man in his cold wet face. The suckers remained stuck so I punched again and again.

Gypsy ran forward and attacked the leg of the fish-man holding me. The fish-man croaked loudly in pain and let go of me.

I leapt back and saw that Gypsy had latched onto the fish-man's leg with her mouth. I noticed blood.

I grabbed onto Ivan to help him pull Christian in. Then a few more fish-men emerged from the water.

The snakes returned. They had flanked the fish-men on each side and were slithering inward three on each side. As they crossed in the middle they formed a curved, living rainbow wall. Their size and numbers forced the additional fish-men back into the water.

The six snakes overtook all but one of the fish people on shore and swiftly wrapped them up in their coils. The single fish-man that remained inside the snake wall had kicked Gypsy onto her back and grabbed Christian again and began to pull.

Ivan and his bother were still being pulled in and I wasn't strong enough to prevent it.

Ivan turned and extended his arm for the fish Christian to sucker on. That gave me an idea. I extended my arm too and Christian attached to my arm too. Firmly attached, I helped Ivan pull his brother up the sandy slope and onto dry dirt. The larger fish-man fell behind and began to claw at his own gills.

Christian let go of our arms and I watched him fall face first onto the dirt. I could see that Christian's gills were working hard but as they dried they stopped. Christian drowned again, on land.

A shadow appeared over Christian so Ivan and I stepped back. Two Angel settled slowly, one over Christian and the other over the fish-man that had been pulling him back in.

The snakes had left six more fish-men dead on the beach. Six more angels swooped in and then settled slowly over their bodies too.

Horace, behind us, said, "I witnessed the entire event for the history folk. And they all agree that nothing similar had been seen in years, perhaps since the rebellion. Nobody ever rescues anyone anymore. We all rely on resurrection. We all are masters of our own fate."

I turned to look at him. "What rebellion?"

"I know it," Ivan said. "We crossed it on our travels. I suppose you could call it a field of the dead, or perhaps a field of the undead. A huge outdoor museum that describes the rebellion with very lifelike exhibits."

The angel lifted off of Christian and he stood there smiling in human form again. Ivan rushed to him and embraced him in a great bear hug. When Ivan released him, Christian looked at all the people and creatures around him and said, "Thank you all for your help. Ivan couldn't have done it himself."

"He's your brother," Ginger the yellow snake said. "I know how devastated I would be if someone took one of my sisters away from me. Family means everything."

"Look," Horace said. "The other angels are lifting."

Two of the others had been resurrected as fish-men and immediately ran back into the river. The first to chase us was the third to be resurrected and bigger than the others. A real strong man of fish-men. He too ran and dove back into the river.

Four women, all wearing fresh clothing, ran up to join the us on the dirt. "Who do we thank," asked the tallest of the four. "We've been down there for what seemed like years. I'm Brightness and," She turned and indicated the three others. "These are my adopted daughters, "Wisdom, Fool, and Haste."

"It was Haste's fault," Fool said.

"We're glad your safe," I said.

Ginger slithered around next to Fool. "I have four sisters," she said.

"Wow," Fool said. "That's a lot of sisters."

"And we never blame each other for anything, no matter what."

"Oh," Fool said.

"We were all constantly pregnant underwater," Brightness said. "And gave birth to fish eggs, millions of them. And we laid eggs about once a week. The males ate the eggs and made a big deal of it because they were a delicacy. But I couldn't bring myself to eat them."

"None of us could," Haste said.

Horace appeared to come out of a daze. He looked at me and said, "There was a rebellion against the immortals in the early days. Back when they were the only immortals and they wanted to make everyone immortal, or at least that how the history is recorded. Some powerful people thought that immortality would destroy religion and they organized armies to fight for mortality, to make immortality optional. One of those early battles took place nearby."

"You have to see the museum," Christian said. "It's the other way, away from the Hop and Fly Festival, but well worth the seeing."

"We'll show you how to get there," Ivan said.

"I hate to be a wet blanket," Brightness said. "Six months ago we were on our way to try to find my new husband. He became a hopper and left for the city. We were following him when we were taken by the fish-men."

Ivan said, "Good luck." The sisters thanked him and set out on their way to find a husband turned into a hopper. I remembered that man jumping high and away when I first woke up. Ah, I thought. That must be a hopper.

I looked at Horace. "You know," I said. "If my dad were alive he'd be proud of me."

"You remember your dad?" Ivan asked.

"He's the only man on the planet that can remember his youth," Horace said.

"And I'm mortal too," I added. My arms hurt and I supposed they would become bruised too. 'Being a hero sucks," I said and wished I could soak away my pain in the river, but didn't dare.

I watched the four women walk away and wondered what it would be like to be trapped under water that way. But I couldn't imagine it.

The women all turned and waved and then Brightness shouted, "You know, there's mostly women down there making eggs for a few bullying men." And then they waved again, a festive wave, and disappeared beyond the bushes.

We all hugged except me because my ribs were still far too sore. "Did you eat the eggs"?" I asked Christian.

"Yes," he said. "They were the only thing that tasted good down there." He began to turn to leave but hesitated. "You know those women lied. They were pregnant all the time because the men raped them. They were too ashamed to tell you that. All the women ate the eggs too. It was all we could eat. Fish, clams, underwater plants, all tasted revolting."

"We should leave," Ivan put his hand on his brother's shoulder. "What's done is done."

Purgatory

We found ourselves facing a tall wall that extend both ways as far as I could see. It looked brand new, but Horace said, "Probably a living wall that keeps regrowing itself."

I craned my neck to look up. "That's a really tall wall."

Writing appeared on the wall and George read it aloud, "Entry to the museum requires everyone agree that no exhibits may be removed. No one may enter until all agree."

"I agree," Horace said. "I guess it is a museum after all."

"I visit every so often," George said. "I don't want to agree but I agree anyway."

The other snakes agreed.

"Me too. I agree," I said.

Gypsy came quickly trotting up and said, a bit out of breath, "I agree too."

Silently, a small hole appeared in the wall and quickly grew larger until a tall and wide archway was present. George slithered rapidly ahead and joined his wives to be first through. We two regular humans and Gypsy followed through last.

Up close, the wall resembled real stone. Interlocked and looking like it had been like that for hundreds of years. On the other side, Gypsy stopped and sniffed the air. Then I smelled it too.

"What is that stink?" I asked and looked around. It reminded me of roadkill.

"A smell added for authenticity?" Horace asked, but nobody answered.

Inside the wall was an area so vast that I couldn't see the far wall. Raggedly broken ground was everywhere. Angels rose and settled all over the land, some far away. And beyond those distant Angels were tiny dots rising and falling like gnats. The area was even more vast than I had first thought.

"Follow me," Ginger called from the edge of a nearby rise.

We followed over broken ground with no sign of a path. We had to detour around scorched metal partly buried and completely unrecognizable. As we crested the rise, we saw George a short ways ahead with the other snakes hanging behind a polite distance. One of the angels lifted off something in front of George so we hurried to see what was going on.

As we passed Ginger she briefly blocked our way and said, "Please try to understand what he's going through. He'd never admit it to outsiders, but he visits here all the time." Then she let us pass.

I arrived first with Horace and Gypsy close behind.

George was in a tight coil watching a wounded soldier. As we drew closer, I could hear George talking to the man on the ground.

"Yes, you're mom's doing fine. She's sorry she couldn't visit." George spoke in gentle tones to the soldier.

I stopped, not wanting to intrude by getting too close. The others gathered around me. The soldier was still in uniform with both his legs had been blown off as if in an explosion, the ground around him had been turned to glass. His bloody, pant legs looked deflated. His gut had been torn open and his intestines dribbled out of his side. One eye was missing and the hole left behind looked burned, smooth and slick. The other eye looked at me and the mouth moved. "Who are you?" His voice sounded flat and weak.

"I'm Puppet." I said.

"Horace stepped forward and waved. "I'm Horace. I'm a historian."

The soldier shifted his eye to look at Horace. "I thought that history was forbidden."

A bloody bubble began to appear at the place in his gut where his intestines hung out.

George looked at Horace. "It always happens the same way."

The bubble grew larger at an alarming rate and then burst. When it did, the air smelled like shit, the soldier screamed in pain. And then his scream was cut off by gurgling blood that began to flow out of his mouth. His one eye moved as if searching for something and then he slumped in death.

George slithered back away from him and looked up.

Over us, one of the angels descended and quickly settled over the soldier. George slithered around to join us. He looked up at Horace and said, "That was my son. A least an Angel told me he was my son."

"Not really your son," Horace said. "We're in a museum. These are exhibits."

"I had been a man like you back then. I believe I saw the war. I must have hidden in the trees and watched it. It may have lasted less than a few seconds or for hours, I don't remember. When it ended, after all the lightening and thunder, there was silence. I tried to run out of the trees and tried to find my son. But a piece of metal had pinned me through my chest to a tree. The Angel, that first resurrected me, told me how I had died, and led me to a body and told me it was my son. He told me how the battle had been waged and that the losers were being resurrected over and over as a form of torture."

The Angel lifted off the soldier in font of us and flew away. The soldier looked around with his one eye, saw the snake and said, "Hi again."

I walked over to the soldier and knelt next to him. "I'm Puppet," I said.

"I remember," the soldier said.

"What do you wish for?" I asked him.

"To die," the soldier said. "Most days I come back to my endless pain and there is nobody visiting. I get really tired of being alone all the time and hurting and dying over and over again and never really dying."

I saw the bubble forming.

The soldier said, "I'm sorry about the sounds I make."

I felt a hand on my shoulder and looked up. It was Horace who said, "We better step back."

I moved away as the solder screamed in pain again and stank again and died again and the Angel settled over him again.

I turned to Horace and asked, "Who's responsible?"

"I always thought it was a museum," Horace said. He was turning in place taking it all in. "I never knew it was real. I really didn't."

George said, "It was the Counsel of Immortals. I wouldn't put anything past them. I'm certain they created this as a warning that no one should ever attack them again."

Gypsy said, "I always thought the Immortals made me intelligent. But could never find out for certain one way or the other."

All George's wives slithered up to join us. George said good-bye to his son and than came over to the others. "We should go," he said. "I can never stay long."

"To the Hop and Fly Festival," I said. "A nice fair would help us all take our mind off of our troubles."

"Yes a fair," Gypsy said. "Why do humans always want to play?"

"I don't know," I said. "In the old days humans loved to play with dogs."

"How did they play with dogs?"

"You know. Fetching a stick. Or chasing a ball into the ocean. Or running alongside a bicycle."

"Why would I do any of those things?" She asked as we exited thorough the arch.

"For fun," I said. "I like to catch balls. I like to catch and throw a frisbee. Wouldn't you like that too?

Ginger's yellow slipped rapidly past us followed by George's red.

Horace hurried up to us.

"What happened," I asked.

"They had a fight," Horace said.

Back To The Clearing

The river still lay ahead. It was late in the afternoon and a few lazy clouds had moved in. A buzz of insects had grown gradually louder, almost a buzzing hum, distinct in the grassland surrounding us. Beyond the grassland dense tall bushes grew peppered with tiny red berries.

"Why would the immortals do such a terrible thing?" I asked George as we came to a stop in the clearing. "I mean, how could they torture people like that, over and over for hundreds of years?" It occurred to me, as I asked that, how comfortable I was becoming talking to a snake.

Horace caught up with us a little out of breath. "Sorry," he said. "I was lost monitoring the history group for a while."

I glanced at him. "That's right you have a Soul in your brain."

"You may have one soon too. You have a serious lump growing on your head."

I felt my head and the lump growing there was about the size of a marble. It was smooth like skin and didn't hurt at all. I even felt a little hair on top of it.

"Anyway," Horace continued. "Everything I witnessed has been broadcast to the history group. But the surprising thing is, well, I learned that the story has bled into other groups and families. And apparently millions of people around the world have become outraged. A lot of people out there believed that the museum, and others like it, held exhibits, but nobody had ever been told that the exhibits were living people. George, through his love, shared his son's pain with all of us. So the world finally realized his son was real. Finally realized that all the people there could be real."

A thunderous thump followed by a second that I both heard and felt through my feet. Two hopping people landed on the path in front of us. They paused there, rocking on their gigantic legs and huge feet, and waited for the dust to settle and for us to walk up to them. Their legs were so huge that my head only came up to their knees. Normal sized bodies on huge legs, squatting bringing them down to talking level. "Hi," the taller of the two, the one wearing a green vest and green combination bowler hat/helmet waved a friendly greeting. The other was dressed in a totally orange outfit. They were both looking at Horace.

"Are you the people who visited the Mortality War Museum?" The green-dressed one asked as the others of our group stopped a few paces away.

"Horace the historian," I said with a gesture. "And I'm Puppet, the only mortal in the world. And oh." I saw Gypsy trotting up. "Meet Gypsy the dog."

Gypsy looked up at them and asked, "Who are you two?"

The green one doffed his bowler hat. "I'm Jackbee. And my co-jumper is Sallyforth."

"What brings you here?" Horace asked.

"We're both present for the annual Jump and Fly Festival. But then we learned about the War Museum —well all that changed. Instead of the Jump and Fly Festival, we're holding the Jump and Fly and Never Forget Festival."

Two of the furry winged people sailed high overhead, majestic against late afternoon clouds. They waved down at us while flying west, the direction of the museum. Then a dozen more flew over. Then a hundred or so flew over. Then the sky went dark for a moment because so many flew over. My mouth hung open at the spectacle of it.

Jackbee said, "They're flying into the Museum to find out everything they can from the living dead and Angels there. Their names, their parent's names, their children's names, where they were from and why they think they should never be forgotten."

George and his wives slithered up as the last of the flying people flew over.

"What's going on?" George asked coiling up his bright red body.

Horace pointed at the last departing flying people. "The Jump and Fly Festival has changed into the Jump and Fly and Never Forget Festival."

Ginger slithered up and quickly surrounded George, hugging him in a snake embrace. "Why the difference," she asked.

"Imagine," George said to her. "If you could live forever trapped in a body that was so terribly wounded you would die over and over from those wounds. For eternity, trapped in repeating your own death over and over. You would never want to be forgotten. Hence the name change."

"Exactly," Jackbee. said. "That's why we changed the theme of the celebration."

George rose up higher to become eye-to-eye with Jackbee. "But why should they suffer so much and forever?"

"That's why we changed the name," Jackbee. said. "So the world would never forget."

Two of the furry flying people landed softly next to the hoppers. Their wings furling up looking spectacular. The older one, with patterned grey and black fur and black wings bowed his head and spoke solemnly. "We spoke the Angel resurrecting Melvin. Melvin's father George, mother Diane, no sisters, one brother Jack who moved to Germany. His only regret, that he will never again see his brother. His one wish, that no one else should ever suffer the same way again."

Ginger slumped down and settled her head on the dirt trail. "We should have told him. I'm his mother Diane."

George said, "I never knew I had another son."

The two furry fliers took off and flew majestically upward to join the thousands of others flying back to the celebration. Then I felt the ground boom as the two hoppers took off.

I turned to Horace. "Do you think we should attend the celebration?"

But instead of answering, he looked behind me and said, "Oh, no."

A snuffler had emerged a short way out of the bushes bordering the clearing. It was behind us so didn't seem to be a threat yet.

Horace said, "They don't travel alone. The others may be circling around to intercept us."

"I don't think so," I said. "Look at its tentacles." The snuffler stopped and its tentacles lay limply on the ground. "Is it sick?"

"I don't know. I didn't think they could get sick."

"I'll find out what's wrong," I said. "My dad always told me if I can't be brave, act insane." I walked slowly toward the snuffler. I considered waving my arms and banshee, but decided on caution instead.

Horace hurried after me.

Gypsy quickly caught up with us.

I glanced back to see what the snakes were doing. George had his head on the ground talking to Ginger. Ginger's four sisters lay belly-up on the ground radiating like spokes away from her. They were moaning over and over in a kind of a dirge.

I got to the snuffler first and stopped what I judged a safe distance away. The huge vacuum cleaner nose of the beast rippled on the ground with a loud snort and raised dust. I was ready to change my scent again.

Horace stopped next to me.

"It's talking," Gypsy said. "A primitive language but I understand a bit of it."

"What's it saying?" I asked. I noticed we were whispering.

"I get the impression it has lost a brother or a sister. Not dead, but trapped perhaps."

The snuffler beat the dirt again with its nose, raising even more dust.

"Yes," Gypsy said. "It has a sibling that is trapped because something fell on it not far away. A female sibling."

"It's a trap." Horace said.

I turned to face him. "But if the other one is really hurt," I said. "Don't we have to help?"

"When you help your enemy," Horace said. "You make your enemy stronger."

I turned back to face the snuffler. "When you help your enemy, you show the world how good you are and how terrible you enemy is. It's a question of perspective. You can only tell how big something is by setting something normal sized in front of it. You can only tell how evil an enemy is by placing something good, and moral and kind in front of it. To compare. To contrast."

The snuffler exhaled harder against the dirt.

"It says that its mate, I think that's right, yes it said mate, not sibling, is trapped and hurt. It also says that without help it would rather die than live alone."

"It's a beast," Howard said.

George and Ginger slithered up on our left. But I thought of Ginger, now, as really Diane, mother of a soldier who had been tortured for over two-hundred years.

Ginger said, "We'll help too."

The four sisters slithered up on our right.

The snuffler raised its tentacles, but instead of reaching forward toward us, it reached behind itself and use them to force aside a squeal and cracking of bushes, which allowed it to turn. When it had fully turned, its backside looked like that of an elephant but with squatter and wider feet. It began to walk and as it walked it left behind a path that was beaten down and fairly smooth.

The snakes followed first, all in parallel, once again evoking the image of a rainbow.

We humans and Gypsy followed a safe distance behind.

Stuck Snuffler

"Long ago there were books that spoke about the difference between good and bad," Horace said. "But once all things became possible the difference became fuzzy and those books fell out of favor."

"I always thought," I said. "That religion was created to frighten people into a moral view that seldom kept up with the morals of society. Religion preached it was okay to have slaves, that it was okay to massacre indians, that it was okay to occupy other counties, that the world was the center of the universe. Religion was always slowest to admit that it was wrong and to change with times."

"Maybe," Horace said. "But didn't immortality co-opt religion?"

"No," I said. "Immortality is only an illusion. I cannot conceive of living a million years or a billion years or a trillion years. Eventually life will become boring and then surely everyone should have the right to die."

"But you don't have to be you," Horace said. "You can live for a while as a man, then change into something that flies and lives in the heights, the change into a snake like George. The only thing that could bore you would be running out of possibilities. And we keep dreaming up new possibilities all the time."

And then we emerged into a wide clearing at the foot of a tall cliff. A huge, wedge-shaped stone had fallen off the face of the cliff and pinned one of the snufflers to the ground. It too exhibited lax tentacles. It's high pitched wail, that we had been hearing as we walked. was replaced by a low rumble when it saw us.

Horace and I walked carefully around the downed snuffler, staying clear of its tentacles. There, held down by one of the heavy but unmoving tentacles, was Windy3. She shouted, "Help me."

Horace and I rushed up to her and, working together, managed to pull her free.

She brushed dirt off herself, then she gave me warm hug and an unexpectedly long kiss. I hugged her back, but then she pulled away and stepped back,

"We shouldn't save the creature," she said.

"Yes we have to," I said, but her callous indifference bothered me. So I walked to the slab of stone trapping the snuffler. I looked it over and said, "That slab of stone doesn't look too heavy." I leaned under one end of the slab and tried to push it up with my shoulder, but the slab didn't budge. "Ah," I said as I stood again, "I think we need a lever."

Horace pointed across the clearing, "How about that tree."

A tree had fallen part way into the clearing and seemed to be fairly free of branches. "Maybe," I said. I looked back and forth between the stone and the toppled tree. "How about we use that rock there as a fulcrum?" I pointed at another flat rock that had fallen a short ways distant from the first.

Horace looked back and forth too. "How are we going to move it?"

Gypsy shouted to us, "I'll take care of it."

Gypsy trotted over to the snuffler that had brought us there. She talked for a short while which seemed to excite the snuffler into waving its tentacles again. It stomped and raised a small cloud of dust. Gypsy led the snuffler to the log and instructed it to pick up the tree at its mid point.

"I can't believe it can lift that tree," I said.

The tree was raised slowly up and over the head of the snuffler leaving behind a roar of falling dirt and gravel. The snuffler began to walk sideway, slowly but steadily toward the fulcrum stone.

I backed up, both to get out of the way and to get into a position to help guide the rescue. Horace had already backed up. Windy3 stayed well away, she had moved to where we had first entered the clearing. She sat on a stump of an old tree, her legs crossed and watched. Despite being held on the ground under snuffler tentacles, her clothing still appeared clean and shiny, and her hair remained perfect.

Overhead a flock of geese flew in formation in the direction of the river. Canada geese if they still had such things. A small bright yellow lizard hurried from one rock to another and vanished as if it had never existed.

With a crashing boom the tree settled onto the fulcrum stone and then there came a banshee cry as the log slid across that stone to the accompaniment of Gypsy's mixed shouts and barks. It slid and slipped as it finally came to rest perfectly under the exposed lip of the fallen stone.

"The angle of the tree is too steep," I said. "There's no way the snuffler can reach up high enough to pull the far end down.

"My turn," George said as he slithered up under the part of the tree nearest the fulcrum. He coiled in place directly under the tree then rose higher and higher until his head could wrap around the tree. "Bark's really rough," he said as the began to pull the rest of his body up to coil around the tree. He pulled his entire body up and moved as far as he could toward the high end of the tree, but the fallen boulder didn't budge.

"I'm next," Ginger said and rose up like George had. She pulled herself up, but as her tail left the ground the tree began to move.

Horace shouted, "I think that's it."

The trapped snuffler made an awful squealing sound.

I back-peddled to get a better view.

The trapped snuffler worked its feet and tentacles and pulled itself out from under the fallen stone. It stood and shook dirt off. The dust smelled like farm dirt behind a tractor.

Horace waved with both hands overhead to the snakes. "Okay," he shouted. "You can come back down.

Ginger got down first. As George gingerly descended, the fallen stone lowered to the ground pulling his end even higher. George was left too high up to lower himself down. So he rose his head up over his body and wound his way back down the tree behind his body, his tail following last.

I backed up gradually while everything happened to get a better view. As George cleared the log and slithered over to join his wife, I noticed the rescued snuffler using her tentacles to remove stuck twigs. A stomping to her left caught her attention next. It was the first snuffler, the one that had led us there. It was waving its tentacles and stomping as if excited. The snuffler to my right let out an ear-splitting honk-honk and then the two snufflers ran toward each other, waving their tentacles as if to hug. But to my dismay, I realized I stood right in the center between the two rapidly running snufflers.

But I needn't have worried. The two snufflers swerved to miss me. Their tentacles entwined and encircled each other, like a continually moving but gigantic plate of spaghetti. I couldn't believe how primitively sexual their movement could look.

A Fateful Flight

Once the two snufflers had settled down, they no longer showed any interest in Windy3. They actually seemed docile and no longer threatening, and appeared more affectionate to each other than anything to fear.

Gypsy asked them to lead us back to the clearing.

They almost looked like two squids caressing each other as they pounded a path ahead of us through the underbrush. The occasional tree fell on the way with a leafy crash.

The snakes followed along the path widened two snuffler widths. I walked with Horace on my right and Windy3 on my left. Gypsy walked behind us, sniffing the air.

"Why are some Immortals called the Counsel of Immortals?" I asked Windy3.

"I can't remember being around more than a couple years ago. But the stories I heard claimed that the Angels were not created by humans. Somehow they appeared when all humanity was dying, and repaired people and wouldn't let them die."

"You mean the Angles are from another planet?" I asked.

Horace chuckled. "Or maybe the moon."

"The story is that people with power and wealth," Windy3 continued. "Decided the world would be better if no one ever died. Those original people called themselves The Counsel Immortals, no one else ever thought the same way. To those original people it was a gift. To most of humanity it was a curse. To live forever and never again have children."

"But why was there a war?" I realized the path being made by the snufflers wasn't all that flat after all. I found myself stumbling over the occasional root or twig or uprooted stone.

Horace pitched into the conversation. "I heard rumors that the war was caused those who ran temples, the ones that believed in a deity that oversaw all human activities."

"I can see how religions might be threatened by a world where nobody could ever die. After all, their beliefs were founded on what happened to people after they died." It felt good to talk and walk. "But when nobody dies, what good it there for theories of an afterlife? I don't believe myself. I've seen too much cruelty to believe any god that would cause such pain and grief in the world. I also believe all religions are wrong."

"That's right," Windy3 said. "It was called God's World War."

We finally emerged back into the clearing where we had started. The sun was half way down on my left and the shadows were long. For some reason I felt like I needed a bath. I was itchy with the collected dirt of too many battles. I was also feeling hungry again.

One thing bothered me. Windy3 said she had only been around for a couple of years. "How old are you?" I asked her.

She shrugged. "I don't really know. Maybe ten or twenty or thirty years. Thirty-six, that's it. Thirty-six years."

Her answer felt contrived to me. "Didn't you tell me you were only three years old?"

She ignored me and hurried ahead.

Two hoppers were waiting for us as we finally arrived back in the clearing. They both slowly rocked on massive legs. They were different than the ones we saw before. Both were women. One was a little smaller than the other. Reminding me of a mother and a teen-aged daughter. The large one noticed me emerge from the bushes and waddled over to me. "We saw you save the life of a snuffler," she said. "Nobody has ever done anything like that before."

Her companion waddled over to join her and faced me too. They both towering over my head. They were proportion like normal sized people atop huge legs. "You can call me Lightdew," she said. "This is my friend Springroll."

I heard a sound like a cyclone of feathers behind me. Two strong, furry arms encircled me, and tightly held my chest. My already-sore chest muscles shouted in pain. "Ouch," I said.

The two hoppers looked flabbergasted.

"Hey!" I croaked. I felt myself tugged and saw myself leaving the ground. My arms and ribs still hurt and the extra pressure on them made them hurt all the more. I looked up. Two huge blue wings beat with tremendous strength over my head.

"Is this high enough?" a voice said next to my ear. I could feel the man's soft furry face next to mine. His breath was air, no odor at all.

"No, I don't want him to change our world. No, I don't want him to end immortality," the man said. It sounded like a one-sided conversation.

I wondered if I should change my odor into a terrible stink, but no, I was pretty high. I could see the forest and grasslands surrounding me. I didn't want to fall so I decided to keep my odor the same.

I could see the snakes in their rainbow colors becoming smaller and smaller. I saw another snuffler approaching the clearing. "Look out!" I shouted. But I couldn't tell if anyone heard me. One hopper woman jumped to try to save me, but was twenty feet shy of reaching me. Her disappointed face receded back to Earth.

"Maybe higher. Oh? Too high?" the man said.

Far below my two saved snufflers moved to intercept the new larger snuffler that entered the clearing. The new snuffler was twice as big as the others and appeared more energetic. It grabbed Windy3 in its tentacle and raised her high above the others. Facing up at me I could see her talking.

That snuffler that grabbed her, turned to reenter the forest. My two saved snufflers try to stop it but failed and they were both knocked over onto their sides.

The man's arms were incredibly strong holding me around my still sore chest. His pressure on my chest made it hard to breathe. His body smelled like lawn or weeds. Almost sickeningly sweet oder that tickled my nose and made me want to sneeze. But I resisted because I was afraid sneezing might make him drop me.

The flying man started to descend. "Yes, lower, of course."

Below I saw the other, the adult hopper leap towards me. I lost sight of her as the winged person shifted me.

The flying man said, "Yes. If I drop him from here he will die badly and become unrecognizable."

"Why?" I asked him. "Why is it okay to kill someone that will die, when you yourself cannot die? What gives you the right to take what cannot be given back?"

I felt two strong arms grab me around my legs and waist and added mass weighing me down, making my bruised chest hurt even more. "It's me, Springroll," said a voice from below my feet.

The wings over me beat furiously and I was leaned over to see down again. "Windy3!" I shouted. The third, larger snuffler that had grabbed her in its tentacles carried her rapidly through the brush away from the others.

I could feel the wind from the two huge wings beating furiously over me, yet at the same time I could see myself rapidly settling back to the road. I could see detail again. The winged man shouted, "Now!" and let go of me.

I fell and knew I would hit hard so I closed my eyes. But the jumper's legs cushioned my landing like giant springs. I smelled burning feathers and looked up. A small dragon with a human-like head flew after the winged man and sprayed bursts of fire at him from her wing-tips. The jumper lowered me to the ground. I felt good to have my two feet meet the dirt again. My chest and legs hurt like hell and I knew the bruises would be worse.

Gypsy hurried over and said, "A snuffler got Windy3 again."

The jumper that had saved me said, "We're going after that winged man. We need to find out if there are more crazy people like him."

"Both of us," said the younger jumper.

I felt the ground boom as they bounded away in high arcs that ended almost out of sight down the trail. A second bound and they were distant dots and then gone.

I looked at Gypsy. "I know. I saw the whole thing from above as it happened."

"Our two snufflers said they were really sorry," she said. "But that other snuffler was too big for them to protect her."

I walked over to the break in the woods where the snuffler had grabbed her. The trampled path was flat and clear enough to see quite a distance, but it curved in the distance so I couldn't see the snuffler that had taken Windy3.

"Hey," shouted Horace from the other end of the clearing. I turned to look at him. The other snufflers were leaving, walking along the path in the direction of the river.

Horace waved to me. "I can see what the soul on your head sees. It must be ripening."

I felt the top of my head and the bump there was noticeably bigger. It still didn't hurt. I looked out the path again that the snuffler made taking Windy3 away. I imagined her in the past, I imagined her as the impossible girl friend I could never again have. "The hell with it," I said.

I started trotting out the path and found it good to run and took my mind off my chest and the way blood was stippling my shirt from the inside. *I'll save you*, I thought and realized it might be my hunger speaking. I ran faster, and the wind against my face felt good, but it hurt to breath hard, so I slowed to a walk again. The ground was smooth, no roots or twigs to trip on. I could smell the grass and the tress, I could feel insects brush my face. From far behind I heard Gypsy shout, "Where are you going?"

I rounded the turn at the end and noticed that the path became straight again and ran into the distance and curved out of sight again. I could see smoke over the far trees, dark and side-lit by the setting sun. I had to find a bathroom and had the sinking feeling it would be an uncomfortable session in the woods for me. So I tried to run again, keeping my eye peeled for a good break in the woods. Despite my chest hurting, I was surprised that I wasn't getting winded. "Good lungs and heart in my weird body," I said and laughed aloud.

I heard someone shout over my head and looked up.

Hovering overhead was another dragon, but with a female face, she was saying something about a fire. I slowed but didn't want to stop. I felt a crazy desire to finally be doing something on my own.

"I couldn't stop the snuffler," the dragon said, flying lower. "I tried to stop it with fire but I set the forest on fire instead."

I looked ahead and saw flames over the tops of trees ahead. Red fire made a deeper red by the sun setting off to my left. I could smell smoke. In noticed there was a wind blowing toward me from the direction of the fire. Not a strong wind, but enough of a breeze to worry me.

"You need to run away," the dragon lady shouted. "You need to hurry."

Closer, I could see she was from in Asia if that place still existed, or if race mattered anymore. "What's your name?" I shouted.

"Bunny," she said.

I found that funny and smiled.

"And my mate's called Rattle."

I stopped and looked around. The night was falling fast. I couldn't tell which way to run.

"That way," shouted the Bunny the dragon who flew up higher and pointed.

I could hear the fire. The cracking and roar of flames getting closer.

Off to one side I saw a cave open up wide enough for me to fit. I ran toward it, with no idea how a cave could open for me. I got closer and saw the cave was in the trunk of a tree. I bent and dove into the hole. I fell on a soft bed of leaves, rolled and turned to look back. The opening faced a wall of trees and underbrush burning, fierce high flames, loud and hissing.

The opening closed and there was silence. I realized the bump on my head was glowing a little. I saw that I was in a wooden cave. Wood, I realized could burn. "Shit!" I said. "Wood in a fire."

Around me a voice spoke. It was a comically slow speaking voice. "I am Cesar. I chose to live slowly. I've

got a tough insulating shell. I won't burn. you won't
burn."

Outside Again

I must have fallen asleep because the inside of the tree was cool when I awoke. The opening was wide open again. My insides felt weird inside has if I had been cleaned out. I didn't need a bathroom anymore. I could smell charred wood but didn't see any embers or flames, only a warm glow over everything. "Thanks," I said to the tree.

Again, slowly the tree spoke. So slowly it reminded me of that comic LP track, *The Slow Talkers of America.*

"Thank you for nourishing me." His speech was slowing. He almost took a full minute to finish with, "You... are... important."

I crawled outside into an orange glow and realized I was surrounded by stumps of smoldering trees. But the occasional majestic trees was untouched. They all looked like the one that had protected me. "Are you all people that became trees?" I shouted. But there was no answer.

I moved my arms and felt my chest, but the pain was far less than I expected. Still, I moved gingerly.

I heard someone shout, "Puppet!"

I realize that the orange glow I saw was the rising sun. I looked around. A dog and tall man walked through the burned out forest toward me. "Horace!" I waved at them. "Gypsy!"

"Where did the George and his family go?" I asked Horace as soon as he got close enough.

"They escaped across the river," he said. His face and clothes were covered in soot which gave him a sort of hobo look.

Gypsy sniffed my hand. Her fur was singed and there was a small patch of bare skin on her side. Part of the skin was an angry red. "We thought we would be safe," she said. "But the fire was too big and too fast. We ran back to the clearing with the boulders and hid there. A burning stick fell on my side. Horace wasn't burned."

"We watched you through your new soul." Horace said. "Saw you hide inside a tree-man."

"What about your burn." I said to Gypsy. "Why weren't you resurrected?"

"We are only resurrected when we die," Gypsy said. "We heal fast, so I'm not worried."

We began to walk in pursuit of the snuffler and Windy3 again. I looked sideways at Horace. "What do you mean my new Soul?"

"Not really a Soul," he said. "But more of an external eye that anyone in the world can watch through. Although I'm the only one that has done that, so far as I know."

"How do I turn it off?" I felt the top of my head. The lump was almost the size of a ping pong ball. It felt like bone, like an extension of my skull.

"You can't," Horace said.

"What? You mean anyone can spy on what I see and I can't do anything about it. Isn't that like 1984?"

"What's 1984?"

"That's right," I said. "You don't remember famous book. It was a novel by George Orwell in which the government spied on everyone and invented a new language to gradually eliminate concepts."

"Can't happen," Gypsy said.

"Oh, why?" I asked.

"No government."

Food Pig

I need food," I said. "You know. Anything at all."

"I'm hungry too," Horace said.

"Follow me," Gypsy said. She sniffed the air took off at a good trot.

We followed even though my spirit wasn't up to it. I found myself shuffling like a zombie. I almost wanted to mutter, "Brains," but didn't. The day was getting brighter and I could see that the snuffler stomped-down part of the forest looked different from the burned part. It was browned by the heat, but not burned. I also noticed that the snuffler had turned to avoid the human trees. That's why, I realized, the path would run straight and then curve.

Gypsy called out, "I found food."

Gypsy came trotting up to us in the company of a modest pig. But the pig looked grotesquely wrong. It was covered in cancers. Large lumps all over its skin, large mushroom and balloon shaped lumps in muted colors.

"Oh good," Horace said. "A food pig. I haven't seen one in over 100 years. I thought they might be extinct."

The pig stopped at our feet and Horace reached down an plucked off a growth off the pig. He took a bite out of it and said, "Potato." He chewed a bit and said, "With butter and salt."

Gypsy looked up at me and explained. "The food pig is covered with nourishing food, but that food irritates it. If it can't find humans or animals to eat its food, it will find a tree to rub the food off and sometimes fatally injure itself. When we eat its food, we give it relief."

Horace pulled off another chunk. Gypsy bit off a piece too. She chewed and swallowed the food. I watched the pig. Each time a chunk was pulled off, it seemed to relax more.

I was so hungry I tried too. I grabbed a black balloon shape and it pulled it off effortlessly. The chunk of flesh was warm. Not animal warm but oven warm. I lifted it to my nose. "Apple pie," I said. I took a bite. Yes it was apple pie, even the texture inside my mouth was right.

It wasn't long before the pig was asleep near our feet, its skin completely cleared of irritating food.

I felt better and less tense having eaten. "I still intend to follow Windy3," I said. "You can't talk me out of it."

"I thought you would," Horace said, wiping his mouth with a sleeve. "I heard from George. He said that the bridge over the river burned so they, and the two snufflers, are paralleling us on the other side of the river.

"Fish," Gypsy said, licking her mouth. "That last piece tasted like wild salmon."

Our walk though the burned out forest was surreal. Blackened bushes and bare trees everywhere. In the distance I saw an angel descend over the stump of a tree. Probably a tree that handn't anticipated fire.

We passed green bits of shrubbery. Why the fire had spared one growth was impossible to tell. A random bit of luck in a forest that was otherwise destroyed.

"The world saw that tree save you," Horace said.

"His name was Cesar," I said.

"The world knows a few forms of life are trying to kill you. Yet many more are trying to save you."

"Why?"

Horace looked at me with a frown. "Why did the tree say you were important?"

"I don't know," I kept walking with no idea how far I had to go. "Maybe being the only mortal person in the world means something." I could almost envision a small car driving ahead of us and thousand clowns tumbling out. Among them my dad who would pause and wave at me. I really needed that. Someone to pause and wave at me, someone that mattered.

We walked slowly around another bend and ahead, not far ahead were two people juggling, a man and a woman. They both had four arms each and, oddly, keep dropping a ball or two.

"We're the Juggling Two," the woman said once we go close. "We used to be a terrific juggling team. But then we took poison so we could come back with four arms each. The trouble is, we aren't used to our extra arms yet. That's why we have so much trouble juggling."

"I saw a four armed man juggling when I first woke up," I said.

"Are you the one that saved the snufflers?" she asked.

"Me and my friends Horace and Gypsy."

She shook my hand with her lower right hand. "Happy," she said and smiled. "And this handsome man is Rednose."

I thought for a moment that it might not be healthy for me to accept such odd people as-is, but the warmth of her hand dispelled that thought. And besides I had been traveling with snakes and a talking dog. "I used to juggle too," I said.

Happy crossed her upper arms and gestured with her lower arms. "So did we. But then we got our new top arms and everything fell apart."

"When I first learned to juggle," I said. "I tossed a single ball back and forth to train myself before starting to do any exchanges. I had to toss one ball for a week before I realized how to do it correctly."

She raised an eyebrow. "Maybe that's our mistake," she said. "We never trained our new top arms. We assumed they would work. I wonder why we didn't think of that?"

"Sometimes it takes an outsider to point out why you can't learn," I said, pleased with myself. "Sometimes you're too close to a problem to see the answer."

Rednose had been hanging back. "I used to be a lone clown, An act designed to show how loneliness could be funny," he said. "But found doing things as a team was more enjoyable."

"My dad was a clown."

He looked surprised. "You remember your dad? You must really be really old."

I shrugged. "I'm the only mortal man alive. I lived once three hundred years ago and was reborn as the patchwork man you see before you now." I bowed slightly. "I remember my dad, the same way I remember my prior life."

Rednose nodded. "Then," he said and smiled. "You are the only man in the world that remembers who he used to be."

"What do you mean?" That made no sense to me. How could I be the only man who could remember my past?

"The cost of becoming immortal," the former clown said. "Is that all memories of your prior life are gone. The first time you die, you have no Soul in your head, so you're reincarnated without prior memories that first time. After that you have a Soul and can be reincarnated many times and with your memories intact each time."

"What about books?" I asked.

"What do you mean. Books only speak of death and things that used to exist and no longer matter. There is nothing in books that could ever have relevance these days."

"So you see, that's where you're wrong," I said.

"So tell me why you think books may be worthwhile."

"I can explain that," Horace said. "I'm an historian and I recently picked up a book. It was written in ancient English but I could still understand it. At first I thought it was a story about death, but it turned out to be a story about obsession. And I have observed that in my travels. I met a female snake who was obsessed with keeping her identity hidden from her son. I met a flying man who was obsessed with the fear that he might lose his immortality. So you see, books are not useless bobbles, but are in fact the memories we all lost when we became immortal."

Rednose frowned. "I never thought of that."

"I know a building full of books," Happy said.

Gypsy leaned against me. "Sorry to interrupt," she said. "Our friends and the two snufflers are making good progress on the other side of the river. They have already passed us."

"That's right," I said. "We're on a quest to save a woman. Perhaps the daughter of an immortal. And should really head off."

Rednose said, "That can't be. No immortal children have been born since immorality began."

Two Jugglers

The sun had set hours ago as Horace, next to me, and said, "You're quest is having an effect on the world."

"I don't feel like I am on a quest," I said

"What do you mean?" he asked.

"When I think of a quest, I imagine a knight of old conquering lands in search of Christ's chalice. Or of a Hobbit rescuing a ring from a dragon. But if I were that hobbit I would have spent my first three days recovering from blisters not having reached the foot hills and would have ruined the whole story. I'm not really on a quest. I'm an ordinary man wandering a brand new world. Wandering and mostly, well, lost."

Horace tapped my arm. "What about rescuing Wind3?"

"She's more an excuse than a goal."

Horace hesitated. "But you're having a real effect on the world."

"How so?" I asked.

"Thousand of people —who believe the past was worthless and not worth learning— are out searching for books."

"It's not only books," I said. "It's movies too, and magazines and newspapers, and any other clues to the past. And what about art, drawings, photographs, statues and other clues about what it means to be human?"

Horace gazed into space for a moment.

Happy said, "There may be videos there too. I don't know for certain, you see I never got inside. I merely looked in through the windows."

Horace came out of his daze and said, "Some historians in the Southern European Ecosystem have discovered an old mine with scrolls and other ancient writings on them. They were written in no known language but their Souls managed to translate them. They appear to have been written by ancient philosophers. And a group in the Asian Plains Ecosystem have discovered something called the Net that may have been the last means of communication before immortality and our Souls."

I looked up at the hoot of an owl and saw the stars over head. I'd forgotten how amazing the sky looked in back-country darkness with no city lights around. "I see the milky way," I said.

Horace and Rednose paused and looked up too.

"Which part do you call the milky way?" Horace asked.

I pointed. "There," I said moving my arm in an arc. "That bright cloud-like area that runs across the nighttime sky."

"And what is it?" Rednose asked.

I looked at him and couldn't believe it. "Weren't you taught about stars and constellations in school?"

"Maybe," he said but he sounded sad. "I don't know if I ever went to school. I don't remember being in my teens. That's the age I must have been when I became immortal and chose to be stuck there. A twenty years old forever, unable to remember what I learned before."

"Men also visited the moon. Of course after those few moon landings we never went anywhere else," I said to Rednose.

"I never knew that men landed on the moon," Happy said. She sounded sad.

"There's no record of anyone going to the moon," Horace said.

"His name was Neal Armstrong. He was the first man to walk on the moon."

Horace gazed off again then said, "No record of him either."

"Let's go," I said. "There's nothing we can do about what was forgotten. Maybe when we find those books."

A Library

Gypsy said, "I smell something ahead that has that aroma of old-style concrete."

I walked next to her and didn't see anything at first. But then the building seemed to rise silently out of the ground as we got closer. A low building barely waist high, wider than I could see in the dark. The snuffler trail turned right, so I considered that right might be the shortest way around. "I don't see any way in," I said.

Happy said from a ways behind, "Left. That's the way I went to find the door."

Gypsy and I turned left and soon Rednose, Happy, and Horace caught up with us.

"That's odd," I said. "The windows are all crooked, like the whole building is leaning to the left."

"The last time I looked in the windows, I saw thousands and thousands of books on shelves. I tried to break a window with a rock but I couldn't even scratch the glass. There," Happy said. "That's were I found the door."

At the corner of the building, a set of stairs ran down into a rectangular hole that was totally dark at the bottom, except for a few pinpoints of light, all of them red. The stairs leaned like the windows which made them difficult to walk down.

We all walked carefully to the bottom.

The door was almost twice as tall as normal.

"Flash hate," Happy said. "Oh, sorry about swearing. I would have thought someone would have already opened the door." He pulled hard on it. "It's still locked."

Gypsy said, "There a softly glowing hand shape next to the door."

Happy said, "Okay," and then first put one hand then the other into the outline, and repeated with her upper hands. "No luck," she said and stepped back. Rednose and Horace tried next, also with no luck.

I stepped up last. I put my right hand against the plate but it didn't fit, my hand was too small, and the lights still continued to glow red. So I stepped back.

"Try your other hand," Horace said.

So I put my left hand into the oversized outline. A narrow line of red moved down my hand, a small glowing sign said, "DNA Exact Match," and then everything turned green and I heard the door swing open with a soft squeak.

Happy sounded confused when she said, "You did it."

I said to Horace, "Could you find a block or a stump or something to block the door open?"

"Why?" he asked. "Books should belong to the Historians."

"No," I said to him. "These books, if there are any, belong to everyone. The historians have no more right to the information about the past than anyone else. A library belongs to all the people of the world."

"I don't agree," Horace said.

"What were you before you became a historian?"

That caused him to frown and seeing his frown I realized the day was growing lighter.

"I don't know," he said. "I think I have been a historian for most of my life, at least the life I remember."

Gypsy came trotting back down the stairs, which was odd because I hadn't seen her leave. She dropped a modest log on the ground with a loud thump. "Large enough?" she asked.

Lights came on as we entered. Tiny lights like stars in the high ceiling, but bright enough for us to see clearly. We had all stopped together in a line inside the entry. Ahead of us ranged shelves and shelves of what looked like books as far as we could see. I could also see that some of the books had fallen off the shelves. I walked in a ways and picked a book off the floor. It was a book of poetry by a woman I had never heard of, Al-Khansa. At least I thought is was a woman because the face on the cover had long hair. But the book was completely sealed in a thin plastic. I tried to tear off the plastic but is was too strong. "Someone." I said holding out the book. "Went through a great deal of trouble to protect all these books."

Gypsy walked up next to me, leaned against my leg and said, "I heard from Greeleech. He told me that a few people came into his shop yesterday and asked to borrow books."

"Did he give them out?"

"Yes, he also said that you're the one that inspired him to start loaning out his books."

"Listen!" Happy shouted from somewhere further inside.

I found a gap on the shelf next to me and shoved the book back in. Then we rushed downhill along the aisle and came to a chest high table. Rednose was seated in an oversized chair. He stood up as we approached. "Look," he said and pointed at the chair. "A real wooden chair. It doesn't change to fit your bottom."

"You called us down her to see a chair!" I said.

"No, look," he said and lifted a sheet of stiff plastic off the table. He held vertical so we could read it. "It lists hundreds of similar places around the world where books and more have been saved."

I looked at the heading on the sheet. It made no sense, then I realized it was written in ancient English. It read, *The Post Invasion Universal Art and Literature Rescue Project.*

"What invasion?" I asked.

"I think whatever brought the Angles," Gypsy said.

Howard added, "Perhaps they were not made by anyone on Earth."

"I found more!" It was Happy again.

I followed her voice and found her thumbing through hundreds of small square boxes. She pulled one out and held it out to show me. If it hadn't been so tiny I would have sworn it was an LP. But it was vastly smaller than a 78, in fact no more than an inch across. On the front it said, "Burgers, Hot Tuna," and I was embarrassed that I recognized it because it was one of those old records from the sixties I used to play. "It's music,"

Rednose carried it to another table. Several small machines rested on the table. Rednose looked for a machine to put it into. "Ah," he said and slipped the tiny box into a slot. But the box only went part way in and stopped.

"Maybe you have to turn it on." It was Gypsy.

I leaned across and touched a small square button with a red glow in the middle. The glow turned green, and the box sucked in. From all around came the sound of electric guitars being plucked, and then a hard drum beat, and then, "Mamma took the pillow from under my head." I began to tap my feet.

"More and more," it was Rednose this time. Another table further down the aisle, full of screens and more boxes. He pulled a small thing that looked like a flat plug from a box of dozens of similar things. He squinted and read the tiny label, "The collected films of Richard Attenborough."

"There's films on there?" I couldn't believe it.

Rednose found another box with a slot that the plug fit into. A list of film came on one of the screens. I walked around the table, but the screen was thin and flat like a piece of stiff paper, and there was no sign of a projector. I returned to the front when I saw, "Chaplin," and touched it.

I couldn't believe it. A film began to show on that small screen. "Like magic," I said.

Horace trotted up and said, "There are people at the door that want to borrow books."

I couldn't take my eyes off that screen. And then I realized I was being awed by something from the past, which made little sense because I lived in a world filled with more amazing miracles of its own.

"Let's go," I said. "After all, I'm on a quest, no make that a mission —no make that a clumsy excuse— to find Windy3."

Rednose pulled the plug out of the machine and the movie vanished. He carefully put it back into its case and replaced the case onto its shelf. "Okay," he said.

As we hurried back uphill to the door, Hot Tuna still filled the place with music.

Gypsy was at the door but I didn't see anyone else there. "Where are they?" I asked.

"Go up the stairs," she said.

I walked up with Rednose, Happy, and Horace. At the top of the stairs I saw too many people. I expected perhaps a dozen people, but waiting at the top of the stairs were hundreds of people, and beyond them others walked, flew and hopped in.

"I'll stay," Happy said.

"Me too," Rednose said.

"One book, or one record of music, or one movie plug, or one of whatever else you find at time. And they have to bring back what the borrowed to get another. And they need to promise to share everything the borrow with as many people as possible." I looked at Rednose. "Operate it as a library."

Rednose smiled at me. "I will take care of everything and insure it is run as you specify."

I reached out to shake his hand but she reached for my other hand, my left hand. He took it and kissed it.

I didn't know what to make of that but shrugged and said. "Good-bye."

Gypsy and Horace and I began to weave our way through the crowd to continue on our way.

Almost every person we passed took my left hand and kiss it. After the hundredth person did that it finally dawned on me that they weren't kissing *my* hand. I held it up and looked it over. It was my black hand. I wiggled my fingers. They were kissing the hand of the person whose hand was now mine. They were honoring the man —the hand did look a bit modest— or woman that originally owned it. After that I let any-one kiss it who wanted to. I only wished that the owner of the hand could somehow know what a good thing he or she had done.

Baby Eaten By A Wolf

The sun rose slowly over a yet another hazy sky. The morning was still chilly as we came upon a rock wall that rose so high it was at least a dozen times taller then I was. I shaded my eyes with my hand and craned my neck, like a rube in a city, but still couldn't see the top.

Gypsy ran ahead to scout a way through. The snuffler carrying Windy3 had turned right to follow the wall toward the river.

"Say, Horace," I said. "You suppose the mortal man that came ahead of me had the other black hand and would have been able to open that library too?"

"It might make sense in a way. But then what would the first man have had?"

Gypsy came trotting back. "I found a gate," she said. "But we have to hurry because it's only unlocked in the morning. If we cut through we might catchup with the snuffler sooner."

Horace and I trotted after her. I looked up as we ran and the sun didn't look at all that high in the sky to me. High, torn clouds dimmed the day. Perhaps the odd weather was throwing off my sense of time. Then I remembered that had been up all night.

When we got to the gate, the sign on it read, "Please keep the gate closed to prevent wild animals from escaping."

"What wild animals?" I asked Horace, as he held the gate open for me. "Lions, tigers and bears?"

"Maybe wolves, beaver, and deer," Horace said.

I chuckled and ducked through. On the other side was a forest that had not burned out. I could hear birds in the trees and the buzz of insects. The forest looked majestic and felt peaceful. A yellow butterfly lifted off a moss covered log and disappeared back through the dark green underbrush, its wings glistened blue the yellow and back to blue.

"I expect that on the other side of the forest is another gate," Gypsy said as the trotted into the lead again.

"I hope we find it soon," I said and felt sweat drip into my eyes. The forest was really humid, and filled with many more ferns than should live in a forest. "I hope this short cut will put us ahead of the snuffler." I wiped sweat of my forehead and out of my eyes again with my sleeve. "I always wanted to get one of those bird books so I could identify the birds I saw as I traveled, but somehow I never got around to it."

"I rely on my Soul for the same thing," Horace said.

A distant rat-tat-tat, like a slow machine gun sounded somewhere high ahead. Horace said, "That's a Ladder-backed Woodpecker."

"How the hell can you can tell that from the sound?"

"With the help of my Soul, of course."

I heard the birds go quiet. Gypsy came running back. "I chased a wolf off. Do you want to see a baby?"

Horace said, "Yes," and followed Gypsy.

"A baby what?" I asked but by then they were too far ahead of me to answer. I hurried after them and noticed it was generally warmer in the forest, almost tropical but with a insignificant cooling effect from the tall trees.

I caught up to Gypsy and Horace, who stood bent over something. As I got closer it looked like sticks and bloody rags. The smell reminded me of roadkill. But then, as I stepped up next to them I realized it was a human baby that had been mostly eaten. The body was hard to see because it was in a shallow ditch. "What happened?" I asked. A light rain, more a mist really began to fall and the day began to get cooler.

Gypsy glanced at me. "No baby can be born that is immortal. All newborns lack a Soul so can die."

"Long ago," Horace added. "People tried to raise children but they never succeeded because mortal children invariably resented immortal parents, because the children all had someday to die. And add to that the pronounced risk overtaking them in the new world, which caused children to always die young."

"You mean people still have children?" I asked.

"Yes," Gypsy said. "But nobody tries to raise them anymore. Mostly they're discarded like you see. Tossed into the forest to be eaten by wolves."

"And in the cities," Horace said. "People there toss babies over the side and let the road surface recycle them."

I shivered. It seemed plain wrong to me. "You mean that's why I haven't seen any children?"

"Most likely," Gypsy said and added, "We should keep going and try go get out of the forest before night falls."

"Should we bury it?" I asked. But Horace and Gypsy were walking away again. I looked at the pitiable dead baby and wondered if it and I were related. I mean, if only because we could both die. I shook my head and hurried after the others.

The forest didn't seem so picturesque anymore. It began to rain harder and a wind came up. I could hear the trees limbs wildly moving overhead. Instead of sweat I wiped rain from my eyes. Certainly not any-place I would ever want to camp. "A deep dark frighten-ing forest were children are thrown away to die."

A Suburban House

I followed the others a few paces behind thinking about what the present future looked like. Why, I wondered should the price of immortality be that you have to forget the past? The price of immortality is that your children will be mortal. How could a dog like Gypsy be immortal when children cannot? Why were people forced to die over and over again in a museum?

Horace shouted for me to hurry up, so I did and immerged into a narrow clearing, across from which was a series of differently styled fences, each with a gate and each with a house beyond. Like a suburban neighborhood from behind. The rain had slacked off again and the sun peeked out briefly, so everything sparkled with water drops.

A man emerged from a gate two houses to our right. He noticed us and waved.

Horace raised his hand in a formal wave and said, "We're trying to get to the river to follow a snuffler that took a woman."

"Well sure," the man said. "Me and the wife are happy to have any stranger visit." He rubbed his long black beard. "It's been ten years since the last visitor and than had been a woman who resurrected herself as a phoenix. Almost burned down the neighborhood." He rubbed his grizzly beard again and chuckled at his own joke. "Join us for dinner won't you?"

"And maybe someplace to sleep," I said. I felt more tired than I have ever felt before. It was like coming down after being stoned but coming down after being awake instead.

"No problem," the man said. "We have lots of rooms and a couple of the houses next to us are empty too. And a fire going so you can dry yourselves off."

The man introduce himself as Lambda, and his wife Maggs. They both looked like an ex-hippie middle class family like from my own day. He wore round sunglasses and a vest over a gray t-shirt, his beard covered where a tie should be.

She was dressed in what I might have called a washer-woman's dress, white, baggy and almost floor length. We sat around a large oak table with a flower arrangement in its center. Two baskets of fresh baked muffins on either side, the aroma of something good simmering on the stove.

"We hope your dog doesn't mind sitting on a bench to join us." Maggs said.

Gypsy said, "Not at all. I like the cushion," as she hopped up.

Lambda passed the basket of muffins to me. As I took one, he said, "You look odd. Like you're made up of many stitched together parts. Does it hurt?"

"Not at all," I said. "But then I'm not immortal like you."

Maggs began to shake and looked down and actually began to weep. She wiped her eyes with a napkin.

"Who would raise a mortal like you to adulthood?" Lambda asked me and fingered his beard as if nervous.

Horace spoke up, "He wasn't raised. He was created like you see him. But he remembers his past, even his childhood, which is something that none of us do."

"Sorry," Lambda said. "It's, well. . . ."

Maggs let out moan and looked up at me. "Nine," She said and looked away again. "I put nine of my babies into to the trash ever since I became one of the Lost People. Not the first few of course. I tried to raise them, but they always seemed so cold and distant. But then my daughter began to blame me for her being mortal. She demanded to know why I didn't make her immortal too. My son and daughter left home and I never heard from them again. I later heard that my son fell off a road in the city, and my daughter drowned in a river. But I never knew for certain."

"I'm so sorry," I said. "So sorry that I have to be present when your children can't be."

Lambda stood, rubbed his hands together and said, "I'll serve the stew."

Maggs looked at me again. "I don't blame you."

"But," I said. "You still sound bitter. Who do you blame."

She looked like she might spit. "The Counsel of Immortals of course, and the Angels they're in cahoots with."

Horace said, "The Angels saved humanity,"

Lambda began to ladle out stew. "Saved themselves is more like it."

Gypsy said, "Puppet is trying to save an immortal from a snuffler."

"Puppet," Lambda said and ladled stew into my bowl. "Your the one that saved those folks from the fish people. You're the one—" he heaped more stew into my bowl than anyone else. "You saved that trapped snuffler. Your the one in the company of snakes and dragons. You're the one that opened that library."

"That's plenty," I said held my hand over my bowl. I felt a drop of stew fall on the back of my hand. It was pleasantly warm.

Gypsy said, "Your stew smells perfect."

"It's your hand," Maggs said. "The one that opened that door."

I took a sip of stew and it was delicious, full of chunks of vegetables and chunks of some kind of meat. "There were two patchwork mortals before me. Both of them died before getting even a third of the way to you."

"We both died of something called the Cough and were resurrected on the street outside," Lambda said. He set the serving bowl down and sat. "We didn't remember who we were, or what happened before, but I saw her and was in love at once. That was two-hundred ago. That's why we call ourselves the Lost People. Because we can live forever but can't remember anything that happened before."

The stew was delicious. It reminded me of the stew my mom made, but it had larger chunks and whole small potatoes. "My mom died when I was a boy.

I never knew her all that well. I died before my dad did."

"And you remember," Lambda said. "How wonderful that must be."

"I remember because I'm mortal," I said.

"But that lump on your head," Maggs said. "Is that an external Soul?"

Gypsy looked up from her bowl, her whiskers damp. "That's an external eye, so we can keep track of him." She licked her whiskers clean.

Maggs had finished her stew and leaned with both arms on the table. "Can we go with you on your quest?"

Lambda looked at her oddly as he tucked his beard inside his vest to eat. "You want to leave?"

"Other than that boat trip to J-land we've never gone anywhere. Other than to the City to find special foods and clothing, I mean."

"Only nine kids in two-hundred years?" I asked.

"It's weird," she said. "I am fertile only one year out of every fifty years. And I forget the pain and bother of giving birth." she said, as if she were making wish.

Horace appeared lost in thought again. He looked at Maggs and said, "The women in the North Eastern American Ecosystem gave been taking a drug for centuries to prevent all pregnancies."

"I should get some of those," Maggs said.

"I know someone that can help you," Gypsy said. "But you'd have to travel into the City again."

Maggs sat up straight and said, "I could do that."

After dinner, we were shown to the spare rooms were we could sleep. I'm ashamed to say I laid down

fully dressed with my shoes still on and fell asleep
immediately.

Hole In A Wall

The next morning, our small group was joined by Lambda and Maggs. Lambda had cut his beard short for the trip. Maggs wore pants and a long sleeve man's shirt.

We followed the road to a small bridge over a creek and on the other side a forest began. It was not a dense forest, mostly tall pines with smaller trees (maybe spruces) and bushes scattered around seemingly at random. The day was still cloudy, but I was pleased that the rain had ended.

At mid day, after a break of lunch under a small boulder outcropping, with many smaller boulders for seating, we finally reached the snuffler path. A mid-sized pine tree had been knocked over and we had to detour around it. On the other side we found a path of smashed down dirt and plants that ran off to our left.

The path was straight as an arrow over a low hill and then vanished. It was wide enough for all of us to walk side by side. Maggs walked next to me.

"You ever have any kids?" she asked.

"My first wife turned out to be pregnant when she divorced me. I didn't find out until much later after she remarried and moved with her new husband to Japan. The old country I mean. So, no I never had the experience of children."

"I always thought I'd make a great mother. That is until my disaster with mortal children. It seems so damned unfair."

"You ever thought of trying again?"

"Good god no!" She said. "I learned my lesson a long time ago."

"But it makes no sense to me," I said. "Why wouldn't the children of people who are not allowed to die be given the same opportunity?"

Horace, on the other side of Maggs, said, "There are no reports of children being resurrected."

We crested the hill and started down the other side. The path ran straight downhill until it met a wall made of vertical tree trunks near the base of the hill. The log wall looked like an old western military fort. I saw two dozen people working with hand tools to repair a wide break in that wall.

As we neared, two teenaged-looking girls waved at us. The adults said something sharply to them and the girls ran away from us. As we got closer, two of the men walked out to meet us.

"You're not permitted," the taller man said. He more than twice my height but was normally proportioned and didn't move like a giant should. He towered over me.

"What do you mean?" Horace asked.

"We don't allow immortals," the other man said. He was shorter than the other but not by much, so both men towered over us like giants. "That includes any of you that are not allowed to die."

I stepped forward. "You mean you're mortal?"

"Yes, we have a town of five-thousand mortals. Well perhaps a few less. Since that creature crossed our land."

"Oh no!" Maggs said. "Who raised you?"

The shorter tall-man, a studious looking fellow with short cut hair, took off his hat and knelt on one knee to be polite. "My father died last winter from a congested chest," he said. "He was raised by a robot when he was a baby. He became one of the founders."

"My name's Puppet," I extended my hand. "I'm mortal too."

"Puppet?" The bigger giant took a step back. "The snuffler was carrying a woman. She kept shouting that Puppet must save her."

"She's alive?"

"Of course. She's immortal isn't she? Why are you trying to save someone who cannot die?"

"If I'd known you existed," Maggs said. "I would have brought you my babies instead of putting them in the trash."

The shorter giant man said, "We have been rescuing babies from the trash, from forests, from baskets set adrift in rivers."

A middle aged but strong looking woman came hurrying up behind the two men. She, like them, was twice as tall as us. She was dressed in homemade looking, crude clothing. "Pardon us being rude," she said. She stepped between the two men and extended her hand. "I'm Ozonia."

"Puppet," I said and shook her hand. Her hand was not as large as the men's hands and was almost comfortable to shake.

She introduced the two men. "The stub of a man is Petrichor, and the tall handsome one is my husband Geosmin."

"Interesting names," Horace said and stepped forward to shake her hand. He introduced the others including Gypsy.

Gypsy said, "I'm immortal too."

"Well don't that beat all," Ozonia said. "A talking dog, and an immortal dog too. Isn't life too unfair?"

"Puppet is mortal so he can follow the snuffler through our property," Petrichor said.

"Where are our manners?" Ozonia said. She turned and waved to the others in the break. "Bring our guests some lemonade."

"I'm so happy all of you are still alive," Maggs said. She turned her head away rubbed her eye, secretly wiping away a tear.

Horace looked around as if surprised to find himself there. "The others have crossed the river and are at the eastern edge of your compound. We'll join them and meet Puppet on the other side."

One of the teenaged girls walked out with a tray loaded with glasses of what looked like lemonade. It had been years —no make that centuries— since I had my last glass of lemonade. As she neared I could see the glasses themselves appeared made of antique glass, deeply purple in places like antique bottles.

"We should go," Horace said. "We have to take the long way around."

Maggs rushed forward and grabbed Ozonia in a motherly hug. "I'm sorry. I'm sorry," she said.

Her husband Lambda had to pull Maggs away.

As my friends walked off, I felt sad. "See you on the other side," I shouted and waved.

The teenage girl bumped me with her hip. I looked up at her and realized she was only two hands taller than I was. She asked, "Lemonade?

I reached and realized glass was giant sized too.

A Funeral

As I neared the ragged gap in the fence I noticed men using picks and shovels to dig out the stumps left over by the telephone-pole sized trees that had been so violently broken off. The work looked impossibly large and dangerous and the men had hardly freed one stump yet. I stopped and stared at the work. The broken trees were more than a foot across and the men lacked levers and machines There had to be an easier way. And then I had an idea. "Gypsy," I said aloud. "If you can hear me. Please have those two snufflers we saved come and fix the fence."

I didn't hear anything and didn't expect to. But then in the far distance I heard one clear bark. Sooner than I expected, behind me there was the sound of heavy feet coming toward me through the forest. I turned to watch but didn't see anything yet. Behind me I heard shouts of. "Another snuffler! Another snuffler!"

I turned back to face the fence. The men clambered out of and abandoned the holes. The teenage girl ran away with her tray, glasses falling on the grass, dumping lemonade everywhere. Screams and shouts fill the air.

Behind me the heavy feet and loud high-pitched wailing stopped. I turned and found myself not more than three feet from the two snufflers. First one then the other touched my head with a single tentacle, the touch was amazingly gentle. Then they separated and passed me on either side and approached the break in the fence. They wailed and touched each other and the fence. And then one turned and walked a ways back into the forest. The snuffler that remained at the break used its powerful tentacles to pull out stumps. Each stump pulled free with a terrible screech and crack and once freed, that snuffler carried the broken end a good distance from the fence and started a pile. Meanwhile the snuffler in the forest had broken a tree off and stripped the branches off the top and had rubbed both ends smooth against a boulder. One by one the broken stumps were replaced with full length logs, the new ones a little longer and thicker than the original. When they were almost done, the removed stumps formed a neat pyramid, and there remained a gap left for one log to finish filling the gap. The snuffler held that log ways back from the gap and waited.

With a start I realized the snuffler was waiting for me to go through the gap. I hurried forward and paused blew a kiss to both snufflers. They both snuffled a small cloud of dust on the ground. I turned and noticed the dropped glasses. I picked up the three that had not broken and jumped over the gap. Then I backed away far enough to feel safe. I watched the last log set into the gap, and powerful tentacles held a large boulder and pounded it down firmly into the hole. The snufflers emitted their wailing sound and then I heard them walk off, following the others east.

I turned and was startled to find hundreds of giant mortals spread in a wide semicircle watching me.

Ozonia separated from the crowd and approached me. "I don't know how you did that, but I thank you for saving our men from the risk of further injury."

A few people clapped and then many more clapped creating applause. I was tempted to bow but didn't.

"I'd be honored if you would accompany us to the funeral."

"Who died?" I asked and immediately became embarrasses as I remembered the earlier snuffler that broke down the fence.

Ozonia's husband Petrichor joined her and gently took the glasses from my hands and handed then to Ozonia. The crowd parted as we walked through. I looked back and found a dozen teenaged girls following us and giggling among themselves. Beyond them I saw that a few people had approached the repaired wall and touched it as if something magic had happened.

The graveyard was a bit further inland. There were more grave markers there then I expected, all sprinkled among a dozen or so huge oak trees. "Have so many died?"

Petrichor shook his head. "These are not all recent."

As we walked between graves I noticed that some of the gravestones showed date in the 1800's, 1900's, and one or two in the 2000's. "Must be a really old graveyard," I said

"The old graves are empty," Ozonia said.

Petrichor added, "We dug up a few to see what might be left, but there were no bones. It was as if all the bones had been taken."

"To make you," said a girl's voice behind me. I turned. It was the same teenage girl that had carried out the lemonade.

Ozonia said, "Venus, I thought you hated the idea of funerals."

Petrichor said, "Puppet. Say howdy to our daughter Venus. She thinks all immortals are not bad."

"They aren't," I said as we resumed walking. "I've met an awful lot of immortals since I awoke. And most seem no different than most humans I had known. Yes, perhaps a few seemed maladjusted, but most seemed quite normal. I mean, in the old days there were many more screwed up and evil people than there seems to be anymore."

"I heard," Venus said. "That's the Soul in the brain of the immortals. It keeps them from going insane."

"It's not a real Soul," Ozonia said with a bitter edge. "Nothing like the real Essence we have."

Petrichor moved to the other side of me and said softly, "My wife has come to believe in gods."

"The primitive elements of earth, air and water or the planets or something from an old religion?" I asked her, but trailed off as we arrived at the funeral. There were three coffins elevated with wooden slats over three holes. A good sized crowd had formed, including young children which pleased me. Someone was already speaking. Petrichor and Ozonia moved into the crowd to get close. I hung back because I wasn't certain how I should react.

A Loony Bin

Venus stood next to me to watch. After a short while she asked, "Did there used to be crazy people in the old days too?"

I glanced sideways at her. She appeared to be in her late teens or early twenties, a young woman. "Depends on what you mean to be crazy. I knew plenty of people that were hooked on drugs, or booze or cigarettes and couldn't quit no matter how hard they tried. Others were simply depressed or overly neat, or unable to make eye contact. We never called those people crazy, rather we said they were in need of help. I knew a few crazy ones in my day. One was a farmer that had raped and killed a dozen young women because his god told him to. Another was a man back from the war and who thought everyone was out to kill him."

"We have crazy people," she said. "You want to see?"

"Will that be okay with your folks?"

She ran into the crowd and soon she returned. "They know where we're going."

I walked with her along a dirt road with horse dropping in occasional piles. But I saw no horses. I breathed in the farm-like atmosphere. "You know I found a library with thousands of books. I'm sure many of those books would help you folks live a better life."

"My dad heard about it but Mom refused to let him go. She believes that immortals will kill us any chance they get."

"I have met many immortals that have not died again since they were first resurrected. All of them are afraid of dying despite knowing they will be resurrected."

"What I don't understand," she said. "Those Angel machines brought everyone back to life hundreds of years ago, but no longer do that. A tree was hit by lightening and an Angel brought it back to life. Several of the men burned it again. Then next time it came back as a woman who was shown the way out. I was there the second time and asked the Angel why we couldn't be resurrected too, but it ignored me. You can't imagine how small I felt by that machine's silence. Our few remaining robots never ignore us."

We reached a large brick building that looked like an old mansion from the south. We walked up the front stairs and were met by a taciturn man with long blond hair. "Who do you want to see?" he asked.

"My aunt. Her name is Cornstalk."

"Ah," the man said. "Second floor, room seven."

Venus ran up the stairs and down the hall. I followed more slowly because of my uneven legs and because the steps were higher than I expected. I noticed all the doors I passed were locked from the outside with large sliding bolts. I felt like a child again among so many tall doors. I reached the second floor. Venus stood near the end of the hall on tiptoes talking to someone through a doorway. As I approached I heard strange screams and shouts from behind a few of the locked doors. I looked up again and saw Venus was gone. I hurried to the end of the hallway and found one of the doors open. Inside Venus sat on the bed next to her aunt.

I paused in the doorway and watched them. The aunt said, "No patches yet. I watch and wait but no patches yet."

Venus looked up at me and said, "Cornstalk. I'd like you to meet a new mortal. His name is Puppet."

Cornstalk stared at me with her mouth hanging open. Then, all at once, she stood. "Patches," she said. "My patches."

She walked up to me. She was short and a little bent over but still well over my head. She looked down at me and said, "You exist. My patches, you exist." She lightly touched my head.

Venus walked up. "She has been talking about patches for years. That's why mom made her stay here. But when I saw you I hoped you might be the man she meant."

Cornstalk took my left hand, the black one, the one that had opened the library and kissed it. "You," she said and then looked me in my eyes. "You will change the world."

"If I live that long," I said and laughed.

"You mean you're a mortal?" She said and frowned. "Well, that doesn't make any sense." She turned and walked back to her bed, saying over and over, "That makes no sense," and shaking her head.

"No sense at all." She sat and looked up at me. I saw tears in her eyes. She buried her face in her hands and wept. Not as if she were sad, but more like she was crazy and sad.

Venus ran back and jumped onto the bed and threw her arms around her aunt. She hugged her with love and whispered earnestly into her ears.

I turned and walked back down the hallway and back down the stairs by myself. Ozonia and Petrichor joined me on the front steps. "We'll show you the way to the second break," Petrichor said. "But first you have to stay at our first guest house. A hot bath and a soft bed will get you ready for you journey tomorrow."

"You show him," Ozonia said. "I'll see to Venus and Cornstalk."

The guest house was as squat two-story building built from rough hewed wood. "I designed and built it," Petrichor said. "They'll let you stay one night for free. No problem."

"You know," I said to him. "In my day mortals built buildings hundreds of stories high."

"Really?"

"Mortals also traveled to the moon. Landed there at least three times that I remember," I said. "So in my experience, mortals may dream higher dreams than immortals."

"Maybe I should visit that library, despite my wife."

"If you do, tell them you're a mortal friend of Puppet, the man with the black hand that opened the library. They will take great care not to harm you."

Clean And Folded

Soaking in a hot bath felt like such a luxury that I couldn't imagine anything better. The tub was not plumbed but was filled instead with hot buckets of water heated over a fire. The soap was primitive but felt good and smelled like moss when I scrubbed my odd body down. The tub was long enough for me to lay down in and raise my hands over my head. All of my body felt like me, despite every part of me looking so different. I ducked my head under the water, with my eyes shut under soapy water. I imagined I was doped up on LSD and this current entire future was just a psychedelic vision.

I felt footsteps through the tub, so surfaced my head and wiped soapy water from my eyes. It was the lady that ran the place carrying a bundle of cloth.

"A robe and a towel for you," she said, and laid them on the chair next to the tub.

"I didn't catch your name," I said.

"I didn't throw it." She said without expression and turned her back and left the room.

While drying myself I finally had a chance to examine my new body in a mirror. Each different piece of flesh was square. I reminded myself of Raggedy Andy. Even my fingers and toes, ears and lips, and my cock and scrotum were made up of smaller squares all carefully arranged to make me appear, well maybe harmless.

Dinner was in a large common room, but I appeared to be the only guest. I was seated at what I was told was the children's table. I was looking over my water glass which, like the earlier ones was deeply purple glass and bigger than normal glasses, when the lady that ran the place set a basket of sliced bread next to me.

She crossed her arms and said, "There something wrong with the glass?"

"It looks really old."

"We can only use things that were made by mortals. I found these buried in the ruins of an old house behind the cemetery. They cleaned up nice."

I looked around and asked, "Am I the only guest?"

She sighed. "You're the first. Not many mortals traveling yet."

"Yeah," I chuckled. "Just me."

"I'll bring your food," she said with a frown and walked away.

A stooped-over man returned a few minutes later carrying a wooden bowl. He set it down in front of me and set a wooden spoon next to it. "Stew," he said.

"How old are you?" I asked him.

"I turned forty-five," he said. "I'm the oldest man still alive."

"Sit with me," I said and picked up the spoon.

"Well okay," he said and sat away with a seat between us. He looked older than forty-five, more like sixty-five, I thought.

I took a bite and realized I was eating a thick soup. Lots of vegetables and mushroom and chunks of what I thought was beef. "Tastes good," I said and gestured with my spoon.

He nodded.

"Who's the oldest mortal you've ever known?" I asked and began to eat.

"The founder, of course. He was fifty-five when he died."

"I," I said. And then I chewed my food more and swallowed. "I was born in 1955 and died in 1984."

He stared at me, but didn't say anything.

"Then I awoke a week or so ago on a bench in the City. In my unusual body, a body made up of the parts of other people's body parts. Dead people parts." I set my spoon down and rolled up one sleeve to show him that my forearm, elbow and upper arm were from other people.

He stood up and moved to the chair next to me. "That design on your arm. I think I've seen that before."

I looked were he was looking, and I had a tattoo on my forearm. It was a complex design with a snake wrapped around a three-dimensional metallic machine piece.

"I'll be right back," he said, and stood. I realized his stoop actually was from age.

I used a thick slice of bread to sop up the soup and enjoyed the seeds in the bread that made it both old fashioned and crunchy good.

The old man returned with the woman that ran the place. She carried an old book tied with ribbon. She sat on one side of me and the old man sat on the other side of me. "My dad said you have a drawing on your arm."

"Art on skin is called a tattoo,"

"Tattoo," the old man whispered a few times as if trying to memorize the word.

I pulled up my sleeve again.

The woman untied the book and looked at my tattoo and then thumbed through some hand written pages. "There," she said and lifted a page for me to see.

It was the same drawing I had on my arm. The writing was in English that I was pleased I could still read. "The man buried was the man that led the development of self-aware of robots. He got the law passed that required all robots to obey a few rules that prevented them from harming mankind or mankind's environment."

"You can read?" the woman asked.

"Of course," I said. "The book was written back during the century after I was first alive."

"You were resurrected?"

"No. I died in 1984 and woke up in my strange body a few day's ago."

"No Angel? No Soul?"

"No, a mortal like you people."

"What's that on your head," the old man asked.

I felt it. It was the size of a golf ball, but didn't feel like anything extra on my head. "I understand it's an eye so my friends can find me."

The woman touched my arm. "Why is the art on your arm the same as the art on the arm of the man that caused robots to raise our founder."

"My left hand," I said. I held it up. "Was from the man that set up a library that could last hundreds of year."

The woman frowned. "You found a library created by mortals that is controlled by immortals?"

"Good immortals. I am sure they would let you borrow any books you wanted."

"I hate immortals," the old man said.

"So do I," the woman said.

"Why?" I asked them.

The old man frowned and said, "Because they threw us away."

"Because they were ashamed," the woman said. "My mother set me in a basket outside the fence. She left a note, but nobody here could read it." She pulled out slim piece of paper and spread it reverently on the table next to me. Sadly, it was too faded for me to read.

Farmland

Venus sat on the front steps with her back to me. I walked down and marveled at the smell of horse droppings, which reminded me of the circus. I looked around and saw two horses in the distance.

Venus looked back and saw me. She smiled and stood. She was shorter than I remembered, a hand taller not a giant like her parents. "How was your bath?" she asked me. Her hair was down and I realized she had brown hair that matched her eyes.

I looked around and asked, "Which way do I go to find that second break in the wall?"

She pointed with a slightly bent finger and said, "That way. You mind if I walk with you?"

The morning was cool with a few high clouds. I was still wearing a thin shirt, at least a clean shirt, but that left me chilled. The bath had reduced my muscle aches. I remained a bit stiff but no longer hurt. I figured a walk would loosen me up. "Sure," I said. "There's lots that puzzles me about a town of mortals living surrounded by a world of immortals."

She bumped me as we started to walk. "Me too," she said. "Me too."

She smelled of wildness and rain. I wondered how fragrances could do that. I imagined myself smelling like waterfall, like spring water splashing over river rocks.

"How did you do that?" she asked. "How'd you change your you smell."

"My friend Greeleech gave me that ability. He's the same one that gave me a lump on my head, the so-called extra eye."

"Was he immortal?" She matched my pace with ease.

I looked sideways at her. "Of course," I said. "The only mortals I ever met, live in your compound."

We arrived at trampled down dirt that looked like the path of the snuffler had made. It ran straight through a field of crops. In the distance, several farmers dug with hand tools as if trying to replant the destroyed part of the field.

"Are snufflers immortal?" Venus asked.

"No, they can die like us." Walking on the torn up dirt, the soil felt of soft and loamy, so I bent and picked up a handful. It crumbled in my hands. It smelled like good dirt, like hothouse dirt, the kind of dirt I used to buy for my house plants.

"I guess that's why those two snufflers helped fix the fence. Because they feel a kinship with you."

"No," I said and sprinkled the dirt through my fingers. "I saved the life of one of them and I think they were a couple. They were grateful, never expecting anyone to save them."

"That seems like a good story," Venus said as we approached the farmer that had noticed us. Many of the farmers had stopped digging and leaned on shovels and hoes and rakes, and watched us approach. "He's mortal!" she shouted at them.

The nearest one shouted something at the others and they all went back to work. That nearest fellow walked to meet us as we continued to walk toward him. He smiled broadly and held out his hand. "Glad to meet you," he said. "You can call me Plano,"

I kept walking forward and shook his oversized hand. "Puppet," I said and nodded at Venus. "And my friend."

"I saw you feeling the dirt," Plano said.

"Good dirt," I said.

"He's been living with immortals," Venus said.

Plano frowned. "Do you always let your woman speak out of turn?"

Venus squeaked, so I touched her arm. "She's not my woman," I said. "She's a friend and an equal. And besides you're the stranger. I've never met you before. So she can talk and you have to ask me for permission to talk."

"You're a heathen," he said.

"You're a farmer," I said.

He puffed his chest out as if proud. "I work hard so that all the mortals can eat."

I smiled. "Immortals don't have farmers. All their food is free. All cooked by people that love to cook and that only require a smile of appreciation. And there are food pigs that have nourishment growing from their skin, and are grateful when you eat those growths."

"We're not immortals," Plano said.

"In my day," I said and waved my hand to indicate the entire field. "We had mechanized tractors to plow the land and to plant crops. And back then there were only mortals. Yet we built machine to help raise crops and we raised more crops than we could eat, so we shipped those surplus crops to other countries. Once, driving thought Kansas and Missouri, I passed a hundred miles of corn fields. Corn growing so high I couldn't see over the top even from inside my car. And the supply of water seem endless. I must have crossed dozens of wide rivers."

Venus said, "We barely have enough wheat to make bread for everyone."

"Anyway," I said. "I have to follow the path left by the snuffler that came through. It was nice chatting with you."

A Second Break

Once we were clear of the farmers, I paused and looked back. "It's funny," I said. "Of all the immortals I've seen, I don't think I've ever seen any of them working hard. I never saw anyone acting like a boss, telling others what to do."

"Yeah," she said. "I guess we're different in lots of ways."

"So what's wrong with being different?"

"My father said that we have to invent our place in the world for ourselves."

I started walking again. Venus pulled off her backpack and pulled out two thin sandwiches. She held one out for me. "Thanks!" I said.

We walked and ate quietly. When I finished I looked around for pavement to drop my paper wrapper onto. Venus noticed and ask, "What are you looking for."

"In the city you throw you waste on the street and the street eats it."

She plucked the paper wrapper from my hand. "We keep our eyes peeled for a compost pile."

"Say," I said. "What would you do if you were killed and one of those angels brought you back? But the cost of being brought back for the first time was that you couldn't remember anything that happened before that? You would forget everything but your language."

"Forget my parents? Forget my family? Forget where I was born and raised? I would hate losing all those memories."

"That's what happened to every immortal. When they first became immortal they forgot everything that happened in their lives before then."

"I didn't know that."

"That's why there is no knowledge of what happened before. It turns out I'm the only one that remembers how the world used to be."

"That's why you knew of machines on farms. Because you saw them, not because you learned about them."

I smiled. "And I opened a library so others could begin to relearn what was lost."

We passed through fields of crops that were rich with green plants growing in rows. The fertile aroma was almost overpowering. Standing water between the plants caused the warm afternoon air to feel almost too humid. I noticed that the snuffler had overturned what looked like beets.

"Look!" Venus said and pointed. "The fence."

I saw it in the distance. It still looked like a normal sized fence.

Venus kicked a lone beet and sent it tumbling. "Why are you following the rogue snuffler? Are you really trying to save that immortal woman?"

"I'm on a mission."

"That makes no sense," she said and kicked another beet. "How can you save someone that can't die?"

"That's not the point," I said and tried to kick a beet too but missed and only grazed it, sending it skittering sideways into the field. "Even trying to save someone made me a hero in the eyes of my father. I helped him save a boy from a kidnapper."

"Is that what you want be? A hero?"

"Why the hell not? I mean I'm living my last and final life, so why not?"

She touched my arm once. "I'd like to be your friend. I'd like to go with you on your quest."

"Life inside the fence is no fun?"

"No it's not," she said as if she were revealing a secret. "Everyone works too hard, there are too many rules, there's never enough to eat. Some men believe that women are second rate and don't count. Mostly in the farms is where they treat women the worst, but there's almost as many farm people as town people. I mean my parents are trying to mate me off to the apple-grower's son and he's stupid."

"When I was a boy," I said. I could see the gap in the fence. It looked like only one log was missing. "I watched a TV show about a farmer and family. They were pretty strict too."

"What's a TV? Is that like a book?"

"Sort of, but with pictures and sound."

"I can't read or write," Venus said. "Nobody that I know can read or write."

I wanted to ask if she went to school, but there was no word for school in the new language. "How do you learn things?"

We were close enough to the fence so I could see a crowd of people gathered around like before. But the crowd seemed to be made up of mostly tall women.

"My mom and dad taught me everything I ever needed to learn."

"If you had a Soul in your brain it would teach you everything you need to know, even how to read and write."

"Mortals have an Essence."

"What's an Essence?"

She shrugged. "It's what lives on after a mortal dies. At least that's what I was told."

We arrived at the crowd of giant woman. It looked spooky to me. All those women and none of them looking at me. They parted and let me though. But I looked back and saw them plucking at Venus saying things like, "Don't go with that heathen." and, "He's evil, he's poison."

Their plucking and comments were getting serious, so I said to her, "You want to be my companion?"

"Yes!" she said and wrestled herself free.

She joined me at the gap. I looked through and saw both snufflers on the other side. I could hear them stomping and snuffling. One of them held a tall log in its tentacles ready to fill the hole. I helped Venus through the hole.

On the other side I heard Gypsy say, "Hi Venus. I'm Gypsy." And I heard Venus laugh with delight.

A Reunion

I stepped through and found Gypsy, George, and the sister snakes waiting for me. I didn't see Horace. I walked over to join Gypsy and Venus and heard the last log being pounded into the hole. Again I felt it though my feet.

"Gypsy," I said. "Venus is mortal like me and you have to be careful with her."

"We didn't know," the Ginger said as a reminder of what they did to me.

"We know she's mortal," Gypsy said. "Your eye, you know."

I looked around again. "Where's Horace?"

George slithered over. "Horace met another historian. A flying man named Agarian. Oh and hi Venus, I'm George." He unfolded and arm to shake her hand.

"Are you a man or a snake?" Venus asked.

"All man," Ginger said and slithered up next to him.

"I'm a man that chose to be resurrected as a snake."

Venus looked confused. "You can do that?"

"When you die," George said. "The Angel asks you how you want to be resurrected. I chose to be a large snake."

'How about you," Venus asked Gypsy. "Were you a human who became a dog?"

Gypsy shivered like she was trying to shed water. "I was never human. I've always been a dog."

"And you're immortal too?"

I answered her, "There are two types of people. The Counsel of Immortals that live forever and dictate the rules for everyone. And then there's rest of every-one, who —I'm not sure of the difference— are not allowed to die."

"I'm not allowed to die," Gypsy said.

I spotted one of those flying men in the distance and remembered being lifted into the air. I shivered despite the warm air. But as it got closer I saw that the flying man was carrying Horace.

"A flying man!" Venus said as she saw him too.

As the flying man got closer I saw that Horace carried two cloth bags in his free hands. The flying man landed far enough from us to not bother us with the dust raised by his massive wings. Horace brushed himself off then picked up the bags and walked over to us with the flying man beside to him.

"Say hi to Agarian," Horace said as he neared. "He's a historian too."

Agarian said, "We brought dinner."

"But why are you allowed to change your bodies when you're resurrected?" Venus asked, sounding a bit frustrated.

"I have a theory," Agarian. Said, as he was pulling food from the first sack. He handed me thin dough like a tortilla wrapped around other food. He handed Venus the same thing. "I think that originally when people were asked if they wanted to be different when resurrected, they asked for things like more strength, more greater endurance, more sexually attractive bodies and, of course, youth."

"But as time went by," Horace continued the thought. "Some people asked for the ability to fly or the ability to breathe underwater. After that there was no limit what we would ask for."

"One thing bothers me," I said. "When the first people were resurrected, did the Angels wait for everyone to die? Some people must have lived to old lives, and then been resurrected when they eventually died. Wouldn't it have been more efficient to put a Soul in everyone's head, than to only resurrect people when they died. That way, at least a few people would have kept their memories."

"We don't know," Agarian said. "No one has ever had a prolonged conversation with the Angels. So we don't know what their rules are."

Venus looked up from her tortilla roll. She had to swallow before she talked. "That makes no sense," she said. "Why did they make mortals immortal back then, and why did they stop?"

Gypsy bumped me with her wet nose. "The snufflers have offered to give you and your friend a ride. They say the ride will be a lot faster than walking."

"But they's so strong," Venus said. She felt something on her shoulder and looked. One of the snufflers had gently stroked her shoulder. "Oh!" She said. "I guess they can be gentle too."

That roll of food was more filling than I expected. I handed Agarian what I couldn't finish.

"What are you going to do with that?" Venus asked.

Agarian smiled. "When it gets dark I will fly over the mortal compound and drop the leftover food in to their compost piles."

"You've been listen to me," I said.

"Your eye," Horace said. "It keeps us in touch with you."

"I think that's...," Venus hesitated as if she couldn't think of the correct word. "Good."

Agarian handed me and Venus a glass of liquid.

I smelled it. "What is this?"

"Seem's prudent to travel over night," he said. "This will keep you awake a while longer."

A Comfortable Snuffler

The drink had not kept me awake as I expected. Instead I fell asleep and woke up still on the back of the snuffler. The sun up to my right, caused shadows from trees to alternate shade and brightness as we moved.

Riding the snuffler was smoother than I expected, a gentle side to side rocking motion. The fur on its back was softer than the best wool I had ever felt, tangled long fur on a wide flat back, made an easy place to ride. I laid comfortably on my back and watching the trees passing by overhead. The snuffler fur smelled like nothing, reminding me that they were probably created by immortals who likely didn't think smell mattered. Or maybe having no smell was an advantage when finding things with their massive noses. I saw a hawk circling high overhead. Again I wished I could identify birds. I wished I had a Soul that would tell me what kind of a hawk that was, or at least a good pair of binoculars and a bird identifying book. I sighed, regretting not picking up such a book while I was in the library.

I rolled over and looked down at Gypsy. She was still keeping pace with us. She didn't glance up.

I wondered how Venus was doing, so I sat up and looked back. Her snuffler was still keeping about twenty yards or so between us. I shouted back "You okay?"

Side to side motion make her appear to be performing a sexy belly dance while seated. She cupped her hands over her mouth so that her sound would carry, "You don't have to check. I'm still fine. I'm enjoying a comfortable ride."

I noticed a flying man approaching low from behind Venus. I couldn't tell from so far away if was a good or a bad flying man.

I heard Gypsy say, "It's Agarian with breakfast."

Agarian landed the back of the other snuffler and handed Venus a cloth sack of food. She said something I couldn't hear. Agarian took off again with amazing grace. "That's what an angel should look like," I said aloud.

Agarian quickly gained on my snuffler and soon landed next to me. "I bring lunch," he said and handed me a canvas bag. "And thanks for the compliment."

I noticed a third oddly-shaped bag in his hand. "Who's that for?"

He smiled a genuinely amused smile and said, "That's for Gypsy."

I dug through the sack and pulled out an apple. Lunch was an assortment of fresh fruits, vegetables — some I recognized and some I didn't— cheese and a long thin loaf of nut bread. The cheese was so creamy yet tart that I could spread it with my finger on the bread. There was even a small cloth-like napkin in the bag. I was wiping miss-aimed cheese from around my mouth when I noticed the snuffler behind me beginning to wander from side to side. Not by much, a few feet, but it looked damned odd.

"Hey Gypsy," I called over the side. "I think there's something wrong with the other snuffler.

Gypsy said something I didn't understand. My snuffler stopped so quickly I dropped onto my butt and had to hold onto its fur with both hands. Two remaining pieces of fruit and an apple core tumbled past me and off the snuffler's head. A tentacle encircled me and gently lifted me back down onto the dirt. I moved away and noticed the dark eye of the snuffler watching me. When I was clear, my snuffler turned and hurried back to the other one. "Venus!" I shouted. "Hold on!" But I needn't have worried, because my snuffler also lifted her gently to the ground and set her well away.

I ran forward with Gypsy to watch. Gypsy had something strapped to her head so she could eat and walk, like a bag surround her muzzle. When we were close enough, she sat and used her paws to remove the bag.

"Your snuffler is acting sick. But the other one cannot understand why," Gypsy said.

Venus joined me and said, "What happened?"

Gypsy said, "We think your snuffler is sick."

My snuffler ran its tentacles over the other as if trying to soothe it. Finally they separated.

Gypsy perked up her ears. "The other one said it's not too sick to get us to the lake," she said.

My snuffler lifted Venus onto its own head. Then it placed me there too. "Looks like it wants to carry both of us," I said to Venus. She took my hand and we sat together facing forward.

The ill snuffler had to lead so that our snuffler could watch it. The trip wasn't as pleasant because the lead snuffler was too close and raised dust that did not have time to settle before we got to it. I sneezed.

Venus held my napkin over her mouth and nose to keep the dust out. "You know," she said. "I think that snuffler is pregnant."

"Not possible," Gypsy said from below. "The Council of Immortals create all their creatures sexless, unable to procreate."

"I've seen enough pregnant cows and sows and sheep to guess that snuffler is pregnant." Venus said then covered her eyes as a huge cloud of dust enveloped us.

Eventually the other snuffler began to walk straight again so the space between them increased. Venus brushed dust off our snuffler's back. And we both laid on our backs again to watch the world pass by.

"What was the world like the first time you were alive?" she asked.

The Past, According To Me

"The past was good and bad," I said. "Sometimes wonderfully good and sometimes hideously bad. We built giant rockets and used them to send men to walk on the moon, then we built intercontinental rockets with big enough bombs to destroy entire countries. We planned to built rockets to shoot down those rockets. Two world wars were fought that killed millions of people, and diseases that killed millions of people more. We build prisons to place bad people into that murdered and hurt other people. Yet other people murdered many but were never convicted. The rich kept getting richer and the poor kept getting poorer. People with dark skins were considered by many to be less than human. People were hanged from trees because they were the wrong color. Six million jews were put in prison camps and killed with poison gas because their religious beliefs offended madmen. Hundreds of native Americans were hanged and their names forgotten. The worst thing that could ever happen to someone was to be forgotten, to have never existed, to not have mattered at all."

I noticed another hawk circling high overhead. Ah, it was riding thermals.

"But the beauty. Ah the beauty. Celebrations that would last a week like Carnival in Rio. The migration of thousands of animals. Proposes swimming in the bow wave of a ship. And wonderful caring people everywhere. And the music, the dance, the movies, the plays, the acrobats, the artists, the architects with their wonderfully unusual buildings. And even when there's war, or natural disaster, or plague, there are always so many damned good people trying to help, people willing to give up their lives so others could live."

Art Giants

"What are those?" Venus jumped up and pointed off to the side.

I looked too. Giants and huge animals stood posing among the trees of the forest. None of them random. The humans were posed as if important. The animals in mid action as if jumping or trotting or cuddling. Everyone of them seemed vital and critical to something silently unsaid.

Gypsy shouted up to us, "They're sculptures. Statues left by some artist."

"I wish I could trade something for one," Venus said, her eyes wide and watching the statues pass. "One of these would look great in front of our main building. Currently there's only an empty square in front of it."

We passed one close and I was amazed by the detail. It was a naked man in the pose of running, and I was certain I could see individual eye lashes. It looked like stone, or maybe some exotic metal.

Gypsy shouted up again, "Have your men come out and chose one."

"What does she mean?" Venus asked me.

"I you know that food and clothing can be free, so art can be free too. These look so big and heavy that someone would really have love one, love it enough to organize a way to move it. Maybe afterward you can get some men from your village to come out to get one."

She laughed ruefully. "The will never come out to be among immortals."

The last of the statues passed by and a few hundred feet further I felt our snuffler start to slow. I looked ahead and could make out the mirror shine of a lake ahead through the trees.

Quicker than I expected, we emerged from the forest onto the wide shore of a large lake. Our snuffler lifted us both off with two tentacles and set us onto rocky sand. Then the both snufflers turned and walked back toward the forest.

I stood there and held Venus's hand. In the center of the lake stood a huge circular building on stilts arching high over the water. The whole thing looked like a building out of a 1950's science fiction movie. Gleaming glass everywhere and pointless flying arches.

But the edge of the lake was being patrolled by dozens, no make that hundreds of huge snufflers. I noticed thousands of people. They all stood inside the edge of the forest. Clearly everyone was afraid of snufflers.

"Look!" Venus said and pointed into the forest behind us.

I turned and noticed that our two snufflers had vanished into the forest. "What?" I asked.

Gypsy said, "They aren't the brightest of beasts."

"We should probably move into the protection of trees like all the others," I said.

Venus took my arm and hurried with me into the protection of large trees. Gypsy joined us.

We stood there watching the huge snufflers patrolling. Every once in a while a tree got bumped over. Once so close, we heard the crash and someone scream. I gradually felt more and more useless. I wonder if this was how my quest would end. Bored to tears and then crushed by a random tree.

"There," Venus said after a what seemed like an hour. "Our snufflers are coming back."

Then I saw them. The weaved among the trees and emerged from behind high bushes. And between them I saw the last thing I expected to see. A baby snuffler walked between them. Not more than a yard tall. It was actually cute.

"A baby," Venus said.

Behind us the other snufflers that patrolled the lake beach began to make strange warbling noises. I turned to look and saw the snufflers on the far shore acted upset too. There waved their tentacles at each other and stomped up huge dust clouds. And then the baby emerged from the forest onto the beach for all to see. All the snufflers went quiet. They all turned to face the baby, their tentacles lax.

Our two snufflers stopped at the edge of the forest with the baby between them. The baby waved its small tentacles and made a loud squeak.

The snufflers on the beach all began to stampede toward the baby and its parents. They didn't seem hostile at all, merely in a hurry. I noticed the snufflers on the other side of the lake all entered the water and started to swim toward our side of the lake.

Agarian landed with Horace next to Venus and me. Horace took one look and said, "A baby snuffler. I never thought I'd ever see such thing."

The snufflers were crowding the trees and I heard our tree make a troubling cracking noise.

"We should back up further out of the way," Gypsy said.

Our two snufflers used their tentacles to turn their baby and began to walk slowly back into the forest.

The crowd of snufflers from the beach followed them into the forest. They moved into the forest single file.

"Where are they going," Venus asked.

Gypsy said, "They may intend to use the forest for their home."

"Free range snufflers," I said.

The crowd of snufflers was finally cleared our side the lake as the first of those swimming across came ashore, their thick fur dripped copious amounts of water onto rocky sand. On the far side of the lake hundreds people had emerged from the forest and lined the shore. Fires were lit on the beach. Tents of all colors and sizes were set up. And I saw hopping people arc into the lake and then swim ashore.

"The lake has a waterfall that feeds the river," Horace said. "We saw it from the air. So there are probably no fish people in the lake."

I looked around. "Where are Lambda and Maggs?"

"They worried too much about the town of mortals. Maggs wanted to go to the city and get that drug that prevents births."

"Who are all those people," Venus asked. "Why are they present?"

"Why for Puppet of course," I heard a familiar voice behind me. I turned. One of the dragons had landed there. With his wings folded, he stood our height.

"Are you the dragon that chased that flying man away?"

"Rattle," he said and stuck out a perfectly normal looking hand. "I chose that name on my first day of immortality and have kept it ever since. I took my name from a desert rattle snake."

I shook his hand. "Where is the other dragon, the one that started the forest fire?"

"That's me." A female voice said. A second dragon stepped up beside Rattle.

Rattle said, "My current wife, Bunny. She's still learning how to use her fire."

"Sorry about the forest fire," Bunny said.

"Meet Venus," I indicated her and pulled her forward. "She's a mortal like me."

"Two mortals," Rattle said. "Does she remember the past like you do?"

I smiled. "No she was only born two dozen years ago. There's a whole colony of mortals two day's walk. Thousands of them."

Bunny stepped up to Venus. "Don't worry my dear. We won't do anything that might hurt you."

Venus smiled as if to a private joke. "I'm not worried," she said. "In fact I find everything, well, thrilling."

The last of the snufflers had entered the forest and from all around us people began to emerge from the forest and populate the beach. Tents were set up on our shore and fires started. Music too. The whole atmosphere struck me as festive.

"Venus," I said. "Do you want to try free food and clothing?"

"You bet!" she said.

"I'll help," Gypsy said.

As we walked along the beach I saw centaurs, and more four armed jugglers, more bird faced people, and some that looked like insect and others that looked like graceful aliens. Some people were half animal and half human, others were pure animal. A black sphere about the size of a volleyball floated by, its black rusty metal finish reminded me of movie robots.

We approached a booth that seemed to offer food. Behind me I head a small band playing something that sounded like the Beatles song, "When I'm 64." Music only, no vocals.

The man behind the counter had six arms and was chopping vegetables with amazing skill. He paused and looked at us. His nose looked extra large, perhaps to help with his choice of spices.

"What are you making?" Venus asked.

"Four different vegetable stews," he said as he scooped up dark mushrooms, tomatoes, and something I didn't recognize and dumped them into the middle of four large pots.

We didn't leave so he paused while wiping his six hands with three towels. "Would you like a bowl?"

"I would!" Venus said. "I'm starving. Is it really free?"

He crossed his arms while his remaining arms gathered up more vegetables to chop. "Why would I ask you for anything when I'm doing something that I love to do?"

"Where I come from, we have to earn our meals."

He unfolded his arms and pulled a bowl down from a shelf. His other arms gathered up chopped vegetables and dumped them into the middle pot again. He remove the lid from the pot nearest us and used a ladle to fill the bowl with steaming stew. "There you go," he said. He set the bowl onto the counter. A second pair of arms set a spoon in the bowl and a cloth napkin next to it.

Venus touched the bowl. "It's not hot."

"It's an insulated bowl," he said. "I looked all over the world for the best insulating bowls and found these in, of all places, in a building next to mine in the City. Is that ironic or just a coincidence?"

I smelled the stew and it smelled devine. I declined a bowl because I needed a bathroom before I could eat comfortably.

Gypsy told Venus, "The bowl won't feel hot, but the stew is very hot, so be careful."

Venus carried her bowl over to listen to the music. A group of five normal looking people were playing what looked liked cartoon versions of normal instruments. A long thin guitar, a square violin without strings or bow that sounded like a violin, drums and a banjo-like instrument. What they were playing sounded vaguely Japanese and was a snappy toe-tapper.

A tall svelte woman walked up and said to Venus, "Where did you get those drab clothes my dear?"

Venus looked up from her stew. "My mother handmade my dress."

"Yes," the woman said. "But look at how it doesn't shed dirt. Look at how it doesn't repel stains. how it wrinkles. So sad," she handed Venus a card. "Say Morro sent you."

I thanked the woman who strode away in a short skirt with impossibly long legs wearing knee-length black boots. Her white clothes were indeed spotless. I plucked the card from Venus's hand and read it. "The best clothing ever. Cherry's Clothes."

I looked around and spotted a booth with the sign, "Cherry's Clothes."

"Can you take Venus there?" I asked Gypsy and nodded at the booth. "I have to find a bathroom soon."

Venus was so into her soup that she let Gypsy lead her away without looking back. I looked around but didn't see anything that looked like an outhouse. So I made a mental note of where I was and set off to find relief.

I passed a man with an extra large forehead sitting on a rocking chair in from of a tent reading a book, so I stopped and asked, "Did you check that book out of the library?"

He looked up and me and smiled. "I did. I found it too hard to understand so I killed myself and got resurrected with greater intelligence. I am surprised no one had considered quantum mechanics before now."

I half-remembered quantum mechanics from a radio show, so I gave him a thumbs up and continued my quest for a bathroom.

The tent, when I found it had a sign that read, "Bob's fecal relief."

He was a small round fellow fixing a long clear-glass tube with a strange tool as I approached. "If you need to go," he said without looking at me, "There is no place more comfortable."

I noticed a few doors along the circular back wall of the tent. "Any door?" I asked.

"Of course," he said but still didn't look up. "A door will only appear if a room is empty."

I entered the nearest door and found myself inside a circular white room with no sign of a toilet. I guessed I would have to squat and defecate on the bare floor. I dropped my trousers and went to squat but felt a seat meet my butt. I looked between my legs and saw water in a clear glass basin. I couldn't help myself. I let go with full force and dropped a huge stool. With that thought, I realized that I was still thinking in English and that, 'a huge stool,' in Worldtalk meant someone who betrayed many others.

When I finished I looked around and didn't see toilet paper. I wondered if I would have to use my left hand like in the middle east. I went to stand and felt an oscillating strong stream of warm water scrub my butt. It ended and then a jet of warm air dried me. I finished standing and found the room bare again. I pulled up my pants and felt myself enveloped in a gentle mist that smelled like fresh flowers. I emerged and knew I had experienced possibly the best bathroom ever. "You were right," I said to the man. "What a wonderful bath-room."

The man looked up. "Hey," he said. "Your the one that opened the library."

"Puppet," I said.

We shook hands. "Justbob," he said. "I don't remember why I chose that name."

By the time I got back to Venus she was already dressed in new clothes. Clothing that fit her better and made her look like a true adventuring woman. Even her hair had been cut and styled into a new look that reminded me of movies from the 1920's. She looked older and more experienced. I wondered briefly if I should get new clothing too?

Gypsy saw me first and trotted ahead. "Horace," she said. "Has found a hotel tent where we can stay tonight."

"Okay," I said. "But I'll have to find food on the way."

Venus linked her arm with mine and leaned close. "We can share a room," she whispered close to my ear, her breathe warm.

I looked at her again. In her new clothes she looked positively perfect and as beautiful as before. "I'd like that," I said. "It's been three hundred years since I slept with a woman."

New Day New Duds

I awoke feeling happy, appreciated and rested, and ready for the new day. I shifted my legs over the bed and watched the room expanded enough for me to stand. I noticed that Venus was gone, but I smiled anyway remembering the night before. I had no idea she was so flexible and loving. As I dressed, I asked, "Coffee?" not expecting anything, but a shelf appeared near to the head of the bed with a cup of hot coffee there. It was a strong black coffee, what I needed to start the day. Fully awake and dressed in my shabby but clean clothes I pushed on the wall at the foot of the bed and a door opened letting me out.

The sun had begun to rise and I saw that some people had slept on the beach despite the roughness caused by rocks mixed with sand. The fires had all died out, the aroma last night's meals was caught in a few tendrils of smoke left wafting through the trees. I walked down to the water's edge and looked again at the building at the far end. It appeared deserted, but well maintained and even larger and more menacing than it had the night before. I couldn't tell if that building was where the snuffler's had taken Windy3. Then I noticed an angel. It floated high in the air half way between the building and the shore. It wasn't like the other Angels. It lacked the bowling pin and abstract wings that the others had. Instead it looked more like a black toaster. Flat black with no ornamentation at all. Dead still, it hung in the sky as if nailed to the air.

I heard birds keening in the trees and the distant soft roar of a waterfall. The sun barely peaked over the trees behind me, so that only the top of the building was bright but the rest was still dim. A fish jumped off shore with a splash and then another, and left circular overlapping rings expanding. The beaches were filled with more tents and booths than I saw last night. A few small birds landed nearby and began to peck at dropped food. They looked like small white pigeons to me, but then I knew nothing about birds. I saw someone in the distance swimming out toward the center, and back again. I sipped my coffee and was oddly content.

A powerfully built man was carrying a large cup along the edge of the water. He wore white shorts and a white short-sleeve dress shirt and strapless sandals that somehow managed to remain stuck to the bottom of his feet. He noticed me and nodded. As he came closer he frowned. "Why are you dressed so ragtag?" he asked and walked closer. "Why are you wearing such ugly clothes?"

"I awoke wearing these. I didn't have much choice in the matter."

"And your skin," he sipped his drink as he looked me over. Up close I could see he had a pale white moustache.

"Why did you chose a body like those art people? The ones made up of parts of dead people?"

I sipped my own coffee and noticed a group setting up to play music. "My name's Puppet," I said and held out my hand.

"Not *the* Puppet." he said. "The reason we all gathered?"

"That's me," I said and stepped back in case he might attack me.

"Ah!" he said and smiled. "All the more reason to get you some good clothes. Walk with me. I know some people who can help."

Music started to play behind us as I caught up to him. A thin flute played a gentle tune.

The man was quiet while we walked, which was okay with me, it allowed me to finish my coffee and remember Venus last night and to wake up fully. We arrived at a closed tent. He knocked on it with a gong-gong that sounded as if the tent were made of metal instead of cloth. An opening furled open like cloth and the man led me inside. I ran my hand over the curled cloth and found it soft like canvas.

A woman with the body of an insect was working a complicated loom, weaving a thread that was being exuded from her abdomen. It looked odd, her human face and long blond hair and such an obvious insect like body with stubby wings and a long abdomen. Another woman with a different insect body was using dozens of arms to hand sew together thin fabric. A third woman, her clothing stained different colors, walked up to me and looked me over carefully. "You need good clothes," she said.

I notice she had six arms and used them to measure me three places at a time relaying my sizes to someone unseen behind a cloth divider. She then led me around the divider and pointed at a cloth door. I went in and found myself in a small cloth dressing room. Clothing was piled on a low wooden bench. I got undressed and dressed myself in that new clothing. I pulled on new boots and tried to stand but the new clothing bound across my crotch and kept me form standing straight. I was going to shout out a complaint but then I noticed my clothes were reshaping themselves. I slowly stood straighter and straighter and felt the clothes and the boots reshape themselves into a perfect fit. Everything, the shirt, pants, underwear, socks and boots were all made from the same strangely self fitting, soft white fabric.

I walked out and the woman that had measured me stood there, her antenna checking me out as if they were eyes. "Mm," she said. "White seems to exaggerate your multi-colored body." She pulled a handful of small marble sized balls from a bag on her waist. "Yes," she said. "Almost but not yet perfect." She began to walk slowly around me, throwing marbles at me that contained color. I looked at myself as the colors formed and I was surprised to find them flowing into hard rectangles, no make that three-dimensional box shapes. When she finished I was a dressed in a colorful cubist mosaic of complimentary colors.

The man that had led me there was gone.

"Your fabric will last you a thousand years," she said as she threw the last marble of color. "It repels dirt, is self cleaning and is water proof. It will cool you on a hot day and help warm when its cold outside. If torn it will repair itself. If you trip and fall a hood will form from the collar to protect your head and mittens will form from your cuffs to protect your hands. Although I don't have personal knowledge, I understand it can protect you from lightening and from modest falls, like out of a tree."

I walked over to the woman at the loom. "Thank you for sharing your body with me," I said.

She smiled, a shy but proud smile, and said, "Anything to make the best clothes in the world. I'm toying with the idea of two dozen arms next time." She laughed a delightful laugh and her many hands worked the loom in a way I couldn't follow. "And next time I will create a thread that can bend light, to make the wearer invisible."

Good Egg

By the time I got back to the hotel-tent everyone else was already up. Venus noticed me first and said, "Sharp outfit. I love the colors." Her smile was genuine.

"What's more," I said. "These clothes fit better than anything else I have ever worn."

"Mine too," she said and continued to smile infectiously.

Horace and Rattle walked up. Horace said, "We ate eggs at a place that claimed to make pre-immortality eggs. I wonder if you could try then and let us know if they are really from your time."

I pointed at the lone Angel in the sky. "What's that Angle up to?" I asked.

Rattle said, "That's Ralph. That's the Angle that first resurrected me. He told me that three people had given their lives to save him, including me. And, because of that sacrifice, he was able to cause thousands of Angels to come from his planet to save everyone else."

"You look like you're getting ripe," Horace said and struck the top of my head with the palm of his hand. I heard something like an egg breaking and bits of rubbish fell off my head and rained in front of my eyes.

"That looks lot's better," Venus said. She used her hand to rub the last of rubbish out of my hair and then gently combed my hair with her hands to make me presentable.

I felt my head and found that the formerly huge bump there was now no bigger than pea.

Venus rummaged in a bag I hadn't noticed before and pulled out a small mirror. "Look for yourself," she said.

Gypsy walked up and said, "We need a plan."

I ignored her because I was so taken with the lump on my head, a small polished back half-sphere on the left side. I had to admit it didn't look bad. I brought the mirror closer and saw that there were tiny swirling lights in the bump. A technologically advanced bump, I thought. I smiled and handed Venus back her mirror.

"I'm glad you like it," Venus said.

"Close your eyes," Horace said. "Try to use the eye on your head."

I closed my eyes but nothing happened at once. The suddenly I could see something. I said, "It looks like dirt."

"Concentrate," Horace said. "Move the view with your mind."

I tried to relax and move that image. It shifted and my view gradually moved upward so I could see Venus. I looked a bit less up into her eyes.

"You can see what I can see?" I asked and opened my eyes.

"The world can see what you see through that eye," he said.

I pointed at the Angel. "Why is it up there?" I asked Rattle.

Rattle shook his dragon head, "I really don't know."

"Do we have a plan?" I asked Gypsy.

"Your quest, of course," said Agarian as he walked up.

I noticed his wings seemed to be fluffing themselves on his back without his control. "How did you learn to use your wings?" I asked him.

"I didn't," he said, "They worked from the first time I got them. It's like they know what I want before I know myself."

The snakes slithered up between tents and booths looking like an invasion of a moving rainbow. George arrived first and said, "Wow! I really like your new clothes."

"Breakfast first," I said and looked at Venus. "Plans second."

"Good," Horace said. "I'll lead the way."

I put my arm around Venus and felt her relax into me. I loved the way she moved. The way she talked. The way she would put her hands on her hips when she was thoughtful.

Another Fateful Flight

After breakfast I felt rested, caffeinated, and full. In short, I felt ready for anything. I was surrounded by all my friends again. Agarian repeated his plan to fly me up to the building. George complained that he couldn't fly so he wouldn't be able to help.

"That's the way we behaved in my day," I said. "You get a group of people together and they can't agree on anything."

"I don't want you to go," Venus said. She sounded unhappy. "Why do you need to save an immortal anyway?"

"To create a myth," I said. "To create a new symbol."

Venus put her hands on her hips and seemed to chew on that thought. "Yes. I can see that."

"The only question," I asked. "Is when is the best time to go?" I hoped the answer would be tomorrow or the next day. I was in no hurry to die.

"In another quarter-hour," Rattle said. "The sun will be high enough so that we and fly in with the sun directly behind us."

"I had the same thought," Agarian said.

"Fifteen minutes?" I asked and heard my voice squeak. I took Venus's hand and said, "I need to talk to you in private."

The snakes understood me and cleared a path down to the water. It wasn't what I had in mind but it would do. I led Venus down to the water's edge and a few steps out into the water. I was surprised that my new boots were water proof. I took both her hands.

"The lake feels good," she said.

"I may not survive," I said. "I need to show the immortals that we are better. But that may backfire of course. The Immortals might kill me."

"I know," she said. "No immortal knows what it means to put you life on the line for something you believe in."

I was surprised. "Exactly," I said. I squeezed her hands. "That's what I wanted to tell you. That no matter what happens to me, you and the other mortals have to keep fighting the fight to change their world."

"Change it how?"

I thought about that. "I don't know."

"We have a saying back home," she said. "Nothing is ever so broke it can't be fixed. Not even a fence knocked down by a snuffler."

Gypsy shouted, "Okay Puppet, it's time."

I gave Venus a hug and the best kiss I could muster. And then I turned and walked back up the beach. The water felt too cold. The day seemed too bright. All around me everyone on the beach had stopped and now watched me. I was acutely aware of my own walk. No music to send me off, just silence.

Agarian took time to fit me with a custom harness someone else had build. "The harness will allow me and the two dragons to fly you up there with minimal difficulty." He said. He pointed at a ring above my waist. "Pull that after you land and it will release the harness into three pieces so we can fly up to watch over you."

I took a few minutes to say good-bye to everyone. Horace gave me a big hug. "The best of fortune for the height of folly," he said. I didn't know how to answer that so I broke the hug with a smile and thanked him.

I gave Gypsy a hug and thanked her too. In return she licked my nose which made me smile.

The snakes all took a turn giving me a snake hug. George was last. "Not good-bye," he said. "A brief farewell."

"Say," I said. "How do you move your body? How do you control it?"

"I don't," he said. "It seems to know what I want and does it on its own."

Interesting, I thought. "If I die," I said to him. "Please save my bones at your place and tell the next one what I did."

He shook his head sadly, and slithered away.

Venus gave me a warm hug and kiss. "Stay alive," she whispered warmly in my ear. "Please stay alive."

I felt the two dragons Rattle and his friend attach to my harness. Then I heard Agarian say, "I'm last as usual." And felt him attach to my harness. And then, I was up in the air, suspended by my harness and watched the beach recede. The air felt cooler as I rose. Venus reduced into a small dot of a greater crowd of dots faster than I expected. Overhead, the beating of wings. Agarian whistling a tune I didn't recognize.

The beaches lay in the shape of a horseshoe around the building. They were crowded with tens of thousands of people. Some waved at me, many only watched. I entered the morning sunlight and felt it briefly warm my feet and back. The breeze from the beating wings was more noticeable. I looked forward and saw my shadow move slowly up the building as I moved higher. The place still looked deserted.

I remembered that others could see through the eye atop my head so I closed my eyes and moved it to look at the building. We stopped rising and started to descend. I felt like I was taking an 8mm home movie and thought I should narrate. "The building stills look deserted," I said. "All the windows are covered with curtains or drapes on the inside to keep the sun out. Are immortals really vampires?" I chuckled at the thought.

We angled down towards a large, deep balcony mid-building. The surface of the balcony looked green as if it were covered in grass. We descended toward it faster than I expected, especially after the leisurely ride up. Before I knew it I had descended to within a couple yards of the surface, felt my harness change so I was hanging with my feet straight down and faced the dis-tant end of the balcony. I felt my feet take up my weight on what turned out to be grass.

Above me, Agarian said, "Pull the ring."

I fumbled with it and then yanked it hard and felt the harness drop away. I turned and watched the trio fly away, each carrying a piece of my former harness. I had to shade my eyes to watch because they flew away directly into the sun.

It was absolutely quiet there on that grass. A slight morning breeze jostled my hair. The balcony was so huge I couldn't see any of the beach past is edge. As usual there was no railing to keep people from falling off.

I turned and walked toward the building. I remembered the eye on my head again, so I closed my eyes and moved it to look straight ahead as I walked. "I hope I find Windy3 soon," I said as my own narrator voice again. "Before I starve to death or die of thirst." I regretted not bringing anything for lunch.

I felt tired, as if the entire weight of the world rested on my shoulders. Then I remembered my new clothes and realized I looked more dapper I had ever looked before, either in my original life or my current one. And, well, that was something at least.

The Fiction Of Windy3

After a good fifteen minutes of walking on soft grass, I neared what looked like a wide array of windows with a door in the center. Overhead arched an unusually high ceiling with round panels that glowed so brightly they matched the daylight from outside. As I approached the still-distant door a woman emerged and stood in front of the it. From far away the woman looked like Windy3. I kept walking and as I neared she looked more and more like her. She smiled and walked toward me. She wore a different and more revealing outfit than last time, low slung with a short skirt and something shiny on her feet. She stopped about ten feet away so I stopped too.

I waited for her to say something, but she appeared to be waiting for me. So I said, "You look good, Windy3."

Her smile vanished —as if her thoughts ducked behind another and was gone— "There is no Windy3. I am Windy2. We created the identity of Windy3 as a means to get you further than the other two."

"The other two patchwork men?"

193

"If you mean the men created from parts of dead found in ancient freezers, then yes you could call them patchwork men." Her speech sounded much more confident compared to before.

"Why not call me Frankenstein's monster?"

"We don't know the reference."

"I opened a library."

"That was unexpected."

I crossed my arms. "Who is the 'we' you keep saying. You don't mean the royal we do you?"

Above and behind her, those bright oval things that I thought were windows began to move. The began floating free of the building A dozen and more of the flat panes of glass floated outward and upward away from the wall.

"We," she gestured at the glass forming an inward facing circle above my head level. "Are the Council of Immortals."

One by one, faces appeared on the glass panels, like thin color TV screens no longer attached to the TV's. Upon the largest window that floated behind Windy2 appeared the face of a man with a gray beard and moustache. He looked down at something on his side of the window, which revealed a tattoo of a woman on his bald head. He looked up again and said, "We assigned Windy2 the task of tempting you to follow. But we never believed you could possibly succeed. The entire point was to demonstrate to the world how fragile life actually is and how terrible it is to die. We used you as a lesson in why immortality must remain mandatory."

"Wait a second," I said and held up my hand as if to halt him. "You mean you created me so that I would die as a lesson to the people of the world?"

"Not you in particular of course. We had an Angel create one of you as a mortal each fifty years, each mortal lifetime, and had planned to continue as long as was necessary each fifty years into the future. What we didn't expect was that you would keep risking your life and do so without dying. You failed to cooperate. You weren't intended to be a living hero. You were intended to be a symbolic death." He shrugged. "Of course now we have a village of mortals to deal with."

He talked as if he was a bad actor reading lines off a page. He invested nothing into what he said, his voice lacked any sign of emotion at all. It was like he was bored talking to me.

"Look," I said. "You," I glanced around at the other windowed faces. "All of you. You simply don't get it at all. The whole reason I came to find Windy3 was to show that even a mortal was willing to risk his life to save an immortal."

"That's illogical," it was a woman's voice to my left. "It's not possible to save an immortal because an immortal cannot die."

I ignored her and talked to the man on the largest window. I decided he was in charge. "I rescued a man's brother from the fish people. I rescued a trapped snuffler."

"That was a mistake," Windy2 said.

"Why?"

The man answered. "The snufflers were created without gender and with no means of reproduction. Your rescue caused a protein to manifest that we didn't forsee. That pair changed into two sexes. When the other snuffler's saw that baby, we lost all control over them. They became independent animals. The one carrying Windy2 dropped her and trampled her to death and she had to be resurrected."

"Sorry," I said to Windy2.

"It's an unfortunate part of immortality," she said.

"Still that must have really hurt you."

"Yes," she said. And I finally heard anger in her voice. She pulled what looked like a golden cross from her pocket. She held it up and said, "I plan to hurt you more than you hurt me."

"Not yet," said the man. "First I have to tell you what we plan to do. The conclave of mortals you found will be destroyed and all the mortals killed. The people that help you will be blown to bits and tended that way forever by Angels. And the next mortal we create will have the mind of an idiot." He looked away and then back at me. "We are the only ones that have the right to vote. No one else is allowed to vote. We decide everything.

I stared at him. I expected his white beard to fall off and reveal a Hitler moustache. I asked, "Would you like me to tell you your mistake, or do you want to find out on you own?"

A voice spoke inside my head, "The rules have changed."

I thought, "What?"

The man said, "Our only mistake was to create you."

The voice in my head spoke again, "You know me as Ralph Angel. I set policy for all the Angels."

"No," I said to the man. "Your only mistake was not realizing that a mortal could matter."

"He's yours," The man said and the window began to retreat back into the building. Faces vanished as they past me.

"I'll enjoy hurting you," Windy2 said, and pointed her cross at me.

My Third Fateful Flight

A blinding bolt of lightening came out of Wendy2's cross and threw me backward into the air. Loud thunder echoed all around me as I flew. I rolled to a stop on the grass, a hood protected my head. I sat up and felt mittens on my hands. I was uninjured but dazed and dizzy but I felt as if I had been in a fight.

That's right, I realized, my new clothes would protect me from electricity and from falling. I struggled to stand and saw Windy2 walking toward me. I looked back and found myself only a dozen steps from the edge. I couldn't see the dragons nor the flying man. I heard more bolts of lightening and more thunder below, so I hurried, the best I could, to the edge and looked down. The building attacked everyone on the shore. A mass panic as people rushed back into the forest, bolts of lightening striking everywhere accompanied by a symphony of thunder. It was the worst lightening storm I had ever seen. And totally artificial.

I turned back to Windy2 and yelled at her, "Why? Why do you need to hurt me?"

She smiled and pointed the cross again. Another deafening bright flash and I was thrown into the air again. But I didn't come down on grass, instead I fell downward toward the water.

But then another bolt hit me and then another. Each time I was stopped from falling and then fell again. My muscles were beginning to hurt like hell from being thrown around so hard and so often. Another bolt hit me and then I fell a dozen feet into water. The water must not have been deep because I quickly hit the bottom.

I stood and found myself shoulder deep in water. I looked back at the building and all the lightening bolts had stopped. That is, all but one that arced out directly towards me. The suit protected me from the electricity, but didn't help me when the water suddenly turned boiling hot. I tried to half-swim, half-walk out of that water. The suit expanded like a balloon around me to protect me but lacked enough insulation. My strength quickly sapped away by the extreme heat. I felt like I was being cooked alive. I looked up to see if a cloud had covered the sun as steam rose all around me. A shadow settled it's blackness down over me. Unfortunately I passed out from the pain before it got to me. I gagged on water and then darkness and fading pain.

Big Boy After All

My pain vanished. A voice. That same voice of Ralph Angel that I heard before, said, "The rules have changed. A Soul vote was taken and the overwhelming majority of people voted for change. In past votes only a small minority, the Council of Immortals, bothered to vote, but now ninety-nine in every one hundred voted. New rules have been formed. Mortals are being pre-planted with souls, so when they die they can be resurrected with full memories intact after they die. The museums will fully resurrect any that want to be resurrected. And resurrection is no longer mandatory. Anyone who wants to die will be allowed to."

"Why did they vote to make these new rules?"

"Why? It was you. When people heard through you that only the Council of Immortals could vote, they wondered why. All around the world, people demanded a voice, demanded a vote."

"How could they all watch me?"

"I will show you."

As if in a dream, I was on a hill above what looked like a Chinese city. Huge screens floating all over the city showed same thing. It was me wrestling with the fish people. Next to me on the hill were a couple having a picnic. The woman said, "We can't die, but we are never brave like that." The man nodded and kept watching my fight, so I watched too. After Gypsy bit the leg of the fish-man attached to me I saw myself stumble back and stand there watching stupidly. Ivan had to lunge forward to grab my arm and only then did I begin to pull again. What the hell?

I was on a mountain side above a plain that looked like I was in Africa. Hundreds of flying people flew to the hillside and settled. A few made music on strange instruments that I didn't recognize. Two flying people landed next to me and smelled of sweat and exertion. Did you see that?" one asked the other. The shorter one said, "Yes the way that hand opened that library. That's what we need, a way to learn about our past and how we came to be what we are."

But what I saw projected was different again from what I recalled. I saw myself walking back up the stairs and Horace had to call me all the way back down to try my other hand. I would have left without trying it.

I was under the ocean. Two whale-sized people built like strangely gigantic finned eggs, swam alongside a pod of whales. Somehow they managed to project an image underwater. Like a movie on a screen of water, I watched myself showing a snuffler a fallen tree and explaining how to pick it up and use it as a fulcrum. But wait. I saw myself pointing out the tree to Gypsy. After that I stood back and watched as Gypsy run around and direct the action. One of the eggs blue a profusion of bubbles as if in laughter and headed up to the surface to breathe. The underwater screen vanished.

I had no idea, none at all. That I was such a anti-hero. "The entire world saw me?"

"Only your world," Ralph said. "Ever since the Cough, most humans lack the desire to venture out into other planets or other solar systems or other galaxies. We fear we have damaged the imagination of your people."

"Not so," I said. "When I told them about the moon landing, it was as if it had never happened. There were no science fiction books or movies generally available before we found the libraries, so there was nothing to inspire them."

"We hope that will change," Ralph said. "It is time for your to choose. You have died. You can be resurrected the way you are, or differently. You can be allowed to die if you choose."

I thought about that. "Will I lose my memories?"

"No. The eye on your head was a primitive Soul. I copied the memories from it to your new soul, so your memories will be intact. While not with the fidelity of a true Soul, but good enough."

"Can you make my face look like I did in 1986, but perfect and younger?"

"Of course."

I thought for a moment. "If I wanted to could I be resurrected someplace else? Like on the moon?"

"If that is what you wish. You body would have to be highly modified to live there. There is a small colony of five such people on the moon now, but they seem very unhappy and I expected them to resurrect back on Earth soon."

"No," I said. "I want to say here. That's what I want."

I waited but nothing happened. "That's it," I said.

The blackness lifted off of me. I stood on the beach. My clothing felt too tight again but it soon reformed itself into a perfect fit again. I noticed that the sand next to where I stood had been turned into glass by the lightening. The building still stood at the other end of the lake, and it was unchanged. Behind me I heard a voice ask, "Is that you Puppet?"

I turned and Horace stood there. His coat was pure white, and the Cheshire cat on his forehead was gone. "It's me," I said to him.

He frowned. "Your face has changed. What happened?"

"My face from back in 1986," I said.

"I recognized the clothes," he said and walked up to me. "That was a terrible way to die. The pain went on for a long time. I never want to die again."

He was much shorter and barely came up to my chest. Which was odd because he used to be so tall. "Damn," I said. "People are shorter these days."

Gypsy emerged from the trees and looked like a normally sized dog. She sniffed and them made a bee-line for me. "Puppet," she said as the walked up. "You smell is the same."

I had to bend to pet her.

I saw an Angel lift off a bright red snake. It took a few seconds, almost as it was extruding the snake, tail out first and head last. "George," I said and hurried over to him. I felt like I could walk faster. Gypsy and Horace walked with me. George looked smaller, but he was still a large snake. "George." I said.

"Puppet," he said. "I didn't like dieing that way."

I noticed Ralph Angel on the beach a distance away. Next to it was one of the Angels with the bowling pin and wings on top. Ralph Angel was twice as big as the others. "I get it," I said and began to walk toward the big Angel. "That's why all the people on the world are half sized. All the Angels are half sized."

"Yes, that make sense," Horace said. "That explains why mortals were all so large. Actually they were normal and we have all been shrunken down."

Ralph Angel lifted and Venus stood there facing the water. She looked around and saw my clothes and smiled then frowned. She walked toward me and I walked toward her. I knew I was no longer patchwork so probably looked different.

She stopped two feet from me and said, "You're the same but bigger. You're adult sized. Your face is one face but the rest of you is still patchwork."

I held up my hands and looked at them. They were white and black like before. "Oh no," I said.

She stepped closer. "I like your face," she said and softly touched my cheek with the palm of her hand. She was shorter than me. More the size of a normal young woman.

I pulled her close and kissed her. She kissed me back with unexpected passion. When we broke I still held her and looked at her face. "Did you die?"

She laughed. "No. The Angel put a soul into my brain. It told me that when I do die, I can be resurrected with my memories intact."

"So you're immortal?"

She stepped back. "Not yet. Not until after I die. I mean I might choose to die."

"No," I said.

"The Angel told me something else. Any child born, whether from immortals or mortals will have a soul installed when the baby turns eighteen years old. Children under eighteen can still die, but over eighteen can be resurrected. It has something to do with the brain size." She stood on tip toes and looked at my head. "Bend over."

I did and she felt my head.

"Your eye is gone."

I said, "I know. I have a Soul too." I stood up straight. "Hey," I said. I guess that makes us soul mates."

She laughed and then looked puzzled.

I realized I was willing to make a joke again. A stupid joke sure; I smiled.

All around us thousands of people began to refill the beach. Hundreds of bounding people arced into the water and used their powerful legs to motorboat into shore. The sky filled with flying people and dragons and strange balloon-like people I hadn't seen before. Thousands of ribbons were being strung from shore to shore with the building being used as the center support.

"Listen to your soul."

I looked down and saw Horace pointing at his head.

"Close you eyes and listen to your soul," he said.

I looked at Venus. She closed her eyes.

I closed mine. I heard music starting up nearby. So I concentrated. And then, all at once I heard it. It was voices, all different voices, all of them repeating what Ralph Angel had told me. "The undead soldiers are being given a choice. Mortals are being pre-planted with souls, so when they die they can be resurrected with full memories after they die. And resurrection is no longer mandatory. Anyone who wants to die will be allowed to. And you can be resurrected anywhere, even on the moon or other planets."

I opened my eyes. "I get it," I said. I watched Venus smile with her eyes still closed.

"A celebration," She said.

Off to my left, a dozen people were building a statue of two women out of pieces of metal. The statue was already three times taller than I was. Across the lake a large replica of a mythical castle was being constructed, which looked really odd because dragons were helping to build it. Large boats floated out onto the lake. Some looked like old barges but with elaborate works of art on them. A horse, two wrestling men, an abstract replica of a sun. One of the boats looked like an old time paddle wheeler which made me think of Mark Twain. "Coldest summer," I said. I noticed a large movie screen being setup nearby.

"Want to see a movie?" I asked Venus.

"What's a movie?"

I took her hand and led her toward the screen. Hundreds of other people were also moving toward the screen but when I asked to get past they mumbled, "Puppet," and let me by. The movie began before we got there. It was Star Wars but a Star Wars I had never seen before. By the time we got close enough to sit and watch, I saw the same characters I was familiar with, but they were really old. For some reason I found that sad.

People weaved through the crowd handing out food. When one man got to us with a basket of rolls, I asked, "Do you have popcorn?"

He stared off in space consulting his soul, then he smiled and said, "I'll be right back."

The movie was exciting, but in old English. Venus had trouble following because she wasn't yet good enough at getting her Soul to translate quickly. The film was exciting to watch and the crowds around us cheered or roared or screeched or blew fire. Then the screen began to enlarge itself and then it floated away so we had to turn our heads to keep watching it. It floated in the air out into the center of the lake growing larger all the time until half the people on shore could watch it.

A man tapped me on the arm. "Popcorn?" he asked and handed me a paper bowl filled with popcorn. I was about to thank him when I remembered my previous corn cob. "Mollycorn make best roasted corn cobs," I said.

He smiled broadly and said, "MollyCorn is my adopted sister. That's so wonderfully kind of you to say."

Venus didn't seem to like the popcorn. She frowned only nibbled on a couple kernels. But by the end of the movie she was taking handfuls.

Sitting on the beach, eating popcorn, with a woman I loved. A cool breeze came up so I put my arm around her to keep her warm. It was almost like being home again. Home in the future, I thought. I shivered, but this time not from the cold

Epilog

I was sitting on a comfortable bench. But my eyes were stuck shut, my ears and noses were plugged, so I had to breath through my mouth. The last thing I remembered was escaping from Utah in my uncle's car. He didn't need it anymore because he had already died from the Cough. He and his wife —a stick of a woman that wasn't good enough for him— so I was glad she died. All she ever seemed to eat was cabbage.

My husband lay in the back seat of the car, he was extremely sick from the Cough. Snow was falling lightly. My daughter Sofia seated next to me, praise God, was still healthy. No radio anymore, no stations left on the air. No traffic on the road just the occasional bone-thin deer looking for food in the unnaturally early snow. No snowplows either so I was driving slowly and carefully. My husband made a terrible gagging noise in the back seat.

That sound upset Sofia so much she began to cry. I looked back. Dried blood was under my husband's nose and below his ears and I saw he was clearly dead. I couldn't take my eyes off of him. The car shuddered and rumbled so I whipped my head around and found myself off the road among trees. I pulled the wheel hard in the direction I thought the road might be and we slammed head first into a thick tree. I felt my head jerk hard, white hot with neck pain.

When I woke up, left my arm was broken and my Sofia was curled on the floor and coughing. My heart broke into a million pieces hearing her cough. Somehow I crawled from the car and pulled her out through the passenger door. Her gorgeous blond hair was caked with blood. Her gentle frame shook with uncontrollable coughs. I looked around and saw an industrial building across the road. There were lights on in the building which meant they had power. No one had power anymore, not in Salt Lake City at least, so this must be a federal government place.

I carried Sofia in my left arm through the snow and across the slushy road and through knee-deep snow to the that building. My legs ached by the time I got near, almost more than my broken arm. There was a guard's gate but no one on duty. Sofia gurgled in my arm, twitched once hard, and was still. I screamed. I couldn't help myself. I screamed at the injustice, at God, at the impersonal universe. I walked down that snow covered driveway and screamed over and over and over. I bellowed and honked like a wounded goose about to become winter dinner. Here I was, about to be sacrificed to gods or fates or to the random cruelty of life itself and my husband and daughter were dead and I sensed I would be next.

The front door of the building was locked so I kicked it several times. Finally I sat there on the ice covered path with my back against the freezing door and rocked my Sofia. I rocked her until I coughed and I kept rocking her until I felt near death myself. The door opened behind me and I fell backwards through the door and gagged from pain.

I must have died then. So where am I?

I used my fingers to pull big chunks wax from my ears and nose. I could hear again and what I heard made no sense. I smelled a wide range of smells, some animal, some human, some unknown. Lastly, I peeled my eyes open.

I was seated under a low overhang on a sunny warm day. The overhang reminded me of a transit stop back when buses actually ran. About a dozen or so people were standing in a semicircle watching me. A few were human, but the others looked strangely dis-torted, like half human half creatures. "Who are you?" I asked, confused. "Where am I?"

A woman with four arms stepped forward. "Did you know you are speaking Ancient English?"

"What do you mean ancient?"

"The last English was spoken over three centu-ries ago. Now days everyone speaks Worldtalk."

A man with the head of a bird nodded to get my attention. "Is your name Puppet?"

"No," I said. "It's Zoya. My name means life." I laughed a harsh laugh. "Or death that is. The death of my husband and daughter. My poor Sofia."

"You remember the past," someone said very close to my right ear. I turned to look. A tiger sat on the ground next to me. My head jerked back with fright, but then I noticed the eyes and the mouth. I realized this might be a human in the form of a tiger. "Are you human?"

The tiger face smiled and I marveled at the whiskers, so perfect they couldn't be real. The tiger asked, "Are you ready for your quest?"

About The Author

Bryan Costales wrote the very successful "send-mail" (bat book) for O'Reilly Media, and the novel "Jo" for Fool Church Media. His most recent credits are short stories published in The Banyon Review, Romance Magazine, and the Riptide Journal. Bryan lives in Eugene, Oregon where he dabbles in photography.

www.ingramcontent.com/pod-product-compliance
Lightning Source LLC
Chambersburg PA
CBHW020838260626
47169CB00003B/1044